BOO[KS]
AVA[ILABLE]

CROSS KILL

Along Came a Spider killer Gary Soneji died years ago. But Alex Cross swears he sees Soneji gun down his partner. Is his greatest enemy back from the grave?

ZOO 2

Humans are evolving into a savage new species that could save civilization—or end it. James Patterson's *Zoo* was just the beginning.

THE TRIAL

An accused killer will do anything to disrupt his own trial, including a courtroom shocker that Lindsay Boxer and the Women's Murder Club will never see coming.

LITTLE BLACK DRESS

Can a little black dress change everything? What begins as one woman's fantasy is about to go too far.

LET'S PLAY MAKE-BELIEVE

Christy and Marty just met, and it's love at first sight. Or is it? One of them is playing a dangerous game—and only one will survive.

CHASE

A man falls to his death in an apparent accident....But why does he have the fingerprints of another man who is already dead? Detective Michael Bennett is on the case.

HUNTED

Someone is luring men from the streets to play a mysterious, high-stakes game. Former Special Forces officer David Shelley goes undercover to shut it down—but will he win?

113 MINUTES

Molly Rourke's son has been murdered. Now she'll do whatever it takes to get justice. No one should underestimate a mother's love....

$10,000,000 MARRIAGE PROPOSAL

A mysterious billboard offering $10 million to get married intrigues three single women in LA. But who is Mr. Right...and is he the perfect match for the lucky winner?

FRENCH KISS

It's hard enough to move to a new city, but now everyone French detective Luc Moncrief cares about is being killed off. Welcome to New York.

TAKING THE TITANIC

Posing as newlyweds, two ruthless thieves board the *Titanic* to rob its well-heeled passengers. But an even more shocking plan is afoot....

KILLER CHEF

Caleb Rooney knows how to do two things: run a food truck and solve a murder. When people suddenly start dying of foodborne illnesses, the stakes are higher than ever....

BLACK & BLUE

Detective Harry Blue is determined to take down the serial killer who's abducted several women, but her mission leads to a shocking revelation.

COME AND GET US

When an SUV deliberately runs Miranda Cooper and her husband off a desolate Arizona road, she must run for help alone as his cryptic parting words echo in her head: "Be careful who you trust."

PRIVATE: THE ROYALS

After kidnappers threaten to execute a Royal Family member in front of the Queen, Jack Morgan and his elite team of PIs have just twenty-four hours to stop them. Or heads will roll...literally.

James Patterson's
BOOKSHOTS
Flames

LEARNING TO RIDE

City girl Madeline Harper never wanted to love a cowboy. But rodeo king Tanner Callen might change her mind...and win her heart.

THE McCULLAGH INN IN MAINE

Chelsea O'Kane escapes to Maine to build a new life—until she runs into Jeremy Holland, an old flame....

SACKING THE QUARTERBACK

Attorney Melissa St. James wins every case. Now, when she's up against football superstar Grayson Knight, her heart is on the line, too.

THE MATING SEASON

Documentary ornithologist Sophie Castle is convinced that her heart belongs only to the birds—until she meets her gorgeous cameraman, Rigg Greensman.

THE RETURN

Ashley Montoya was in love with Mack McLeroy in high school—until he broke her heart. But when an accident brings him back home to recover, Ashley can't help but fall into his embrace....

BODYGUARD

Special Agent Abbie Whitmore has only one task: protect Congressman Jonathan Lassiter from a violent cartel's threats. Yet she's never had to do it while falling in love....

DAZZLING: THE DIAMOND TRILOGY, BOOK I

To support her artistic career, Siobhan works at the elite Stone Room in New York City...never expecting to be swept away by Derick Miller.

RADIANT: THE DIAMOND TRILOGY, BOOK II

After an explosive breakup with her billionaire boyfriend, Siobhan moves to Detroit to pursue her art. But Derick isn't ready to give her up.

HOT WINTER NIGHTS

Allie Thatcher moved to Montana to start fresh as the head of the Bear Mountain trauma center. And even though the days are cold, the nights are steamy...especially when she meets search-and-rescue leader Dex Belmont.

IS HARRIET BLUE AS TALENTED A DETECTIVE AS LINDSAY BOXER?

Harriet Blue, the most single-minded detective since Lindsay Boxer, won't rest until she stops a savage killer targeting female university students. But new clues point to a more chilling predator than she could ever have imagined….

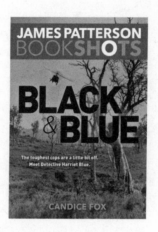

Will Harriet solve the case before time runs out?
Read *Black & Blue,* available only from

BOOK**SHOTS**

THE CHRISTMAS MYSTERY

A DETECTIVE LUC MONCRIEF STORY

James Patterson
with Richard DiLallo

BOOK**SHOTS**

Little, Brown and Company

New York Boston London

Copyright © 2016 by James Patterson

BookShots / Little, Brown and Company
Hachette Book Group
1290 Avenue of the Americas, New York, NY 10104
bookshots.com

First Edition: December 2016

BookShots is an imprint of Little, Brown and Company, a division of Hachette Book Group, Inc. The Little, Brown name and logo are trademarks of Hachette Book Group, Inc. The BookShots name and logo are trademarks of JBP Business, LLC.

The Hachette Speakers Bureau provides a wide range of authors for speaking events. To find out more, go to hachettespeakersbureau.com or call (866) 376-6591.

ISBN 978-0-316-31997-3 / 978-0-316-50631-1 (Walmart edition)
LCCN 2016938306

10 9 8 7 6 5 4 3 2 1

LSC-C

Printed in the United States of America

THE CHRISTMAS MYSTERY

PROLOGUE

ONE

CHAOS AND CONFUSION reign in New York City's most glamorous department store, Bloomingdale's.

A dozen beautiful women—perfect makeup, perfect clothing—are strutting around the first floor, armed. No one escapes these women. They are shooting customers…with spritzes of expensive perfume.

Enough fragrance fills the air to create a lethal cloud of nausea. The effect is somewhere between expensive flower shop and cheap brothel.

"Unbelievable! This place is packed," says K. Burke.

"Yes," I say. "You'd think it was almost Christmas."

"It *is* almost Chris—" Burke begins to say. She stops, then adds, "Don't be a wiseass, Moncrief. We've got a long day ahead of us."

K. Burke and I are police detective partners from Manhattan's Midtown East. Our chief inspector, Nick Elliott, has assigned us to undercover security at this famous and glamorous department store. I told the inspector that I preferred more challenging assignments, "like trapping terrorists and capturing murderers."

Elliott's response?

"Feel free to trap any terrorists or capture any murderers you come across. Meanwhile, keep your eyes open for purse-snatchers and shoplifters."

K. Burke, ever the cooperative pro, said, "I understand, sir."

I said nothing.

In any event, K. Burke and I at this moment are standing in a fog of Caron Poivre and Chanel No. 5 in Bloomingdale's perfume department.

"So, how are we going to split up, Moncrief?" asks Burke.

"You decide," I say. My enthusiasm is not overwhelming.

"Okay," Burke says. "I'll take the second floor…women's designer clothes. Why don't you take high-end gifts? China, crystal, silver."

"May I suggest," I say, "that you take women's designer clothing on the *fourth* floor, not the *second*. Second floor is Donna Karan and Calvin. Fourth floor is Dolce & Gabbana, Prada, Valentino. Much classier."

Burke shakes her head. "It's amazing, the stuff you know."

We test-check the red buttons on our cell phones, the communication keys that give us immediate contact with each other.

Burke says that she'll also notify regular store security and tell them that their special request NYPD patrol is there, as planned.

"I've got to get out of this perfume storm," she says. She's just about to move toward the central escalator when a well-dressed middle-aged woman approaches. The woman speaks directly to Burke.

"Where can I buy one of these?" the woman says.

"I got the last one," Burke says. The woman laughs and walks away.

I'm completely confused. "What was that lady asking about?" I say.

"She was asking about you," Burke says. "As if you didn't know."

Burke walks quickly toward the up escalator.

TWO

WITHIN THREE MINUTES I'm standing in the Fine China and Silver section of Bloomingdale's sixth floor. If there is a problem with the economy in New York City, someone failed to tell the frantic shoppers snapping up Wedgwood soup tureens and sterling silver dinner forks. It's only ten thirty in the morning, yet the line at gift-wrap is already eight customers deep.

My cell phone is connected to hundreds of store security cameras. These cameras are trained on entrance areas, exit doors, credit card registers—all areas where intruders can enter, exit, and operate quickly.

I keep my head still, but my eyes dart around the area. Like Christmas itself, all is calm, all is bright. I make my way through the crowd of wealthy-looking women in fur, prosperous-looking men with five-hundred-dollar cashmere scarves.

Then a loud buzz. Insistent. Urgent. I glance quickly at my phone. The red light. I listen to K. Burke's voice.

"Second floor. Right now," she says. She immediately clicks off.

Damn it. I told her to go to the fourth floor. Burke makes her own decisions.

Within a few seconds I'm at the Bloomingdale's internal staircase. I skip the stairs three at a time. I burst through the second floor door.

Chaos. Screaming. Customers crowding the aisles near the down escalators. Salespeople crouched behind counters.

"Location Monitor" on my cell notifies me that Burke is no longer on the original second floor location. Her new location is men's furnishings—ties, wallets, aftershave. Ground floor.

I reverse my course and rush toward the rear escalator near Third Avenue. I push a few men and women out of my path. Now I'm struggling to execute a classic crazy move—I'm running *down* an escalator that's running *up*.

I land on the floor. I see K. Burke moving quickly past display cases of sweaters and shirts. Burke sees me.

She shouts one word.

"Punks!"

It's a perfect description. In a split second I see two young women—teens probably, both in dark-gray hoodies. The pair open a door marked EMPLOYEES ONLY. They go through. The door closes behind them.

Burke and I almost collide at that door. We know from our surveillance planning that this is one of Bloomingdale's "snare" closets—purposely mismarked to snare shoplifters and muggers on the run. This time it works like a Christmas charm. We enter the small space and see two tough-looking teenage girls—nose piercings, eyebrow piercings, tats, the whole getup. One of them is holding an opened switchblade. I squeeze her wrist between my thumb and index finger. The knife falls to the ground. As K. Burke scoops up the knife, she speaks.

"These two assholes knocked over a woman old enough to be their grandmother and took off with her shopping bag," Burke says. "They also managed to slash her leg—the long way. EMU is taking care of her."

"It ain't us. You're messed up. Look. No shopping bags," one of the girls says. Her voice is arrogant, angry.

"Store security has the shopping bag. And they've got enough video on the two of you to make a feature film," Burke adds.

It's clear to the young thieves that they'll get no place good with Burke. One of them decides to play me.

"Give us a break, man. It probably isn't even us on the video. I know all about this shit. Come on."

I smile at the young lady.

"You know all about this shit? Let me tell you something." I pause for a moment, then continue quietly. "In some cases, with the holidays approaching, I might say: give the kids a warning and release them."

"That'd be way cool," says her friend.

K. Burke looks at me. I know that she's afraid my liberal soft spot is going to erupt.

"But this is not one of those cases," I say.

"Man, no. Why?" asks the girl.

"I believe my colleague summed it up a few minutes ago," I say.

"What the hell?" the girl says.

I answer. "Punks!"

THE CHRISTMAS MYSTERY

CHAPTER 1

Almost Thanksgiving

WHEN DALIA BOAZ died a few months ago, I believed that my own life had ended along with hers.

Friends suggested that, with time, the agony of the loss would diminish.

They were wrong. Day after day I ache for Dalia, the love of my life. Yet life rattles on. Unstoppable. Yes, there are moments when I am joyful. Other times are inevitably heartbreaking: Dalia's birthday, my birthday, the anniversary of a special romantic event. Holidays are a special problem, of course, because I am surrounded by celebration—Easter baskets overflowing, fireworks erupting, bright lights hanging from evergreen trees.

Thanksgiving Day is a unique problem. There is nothing remotely like it in France. When Dalia was alive, if I was not on duty, we stayed in bed and streamed a few movies, whipped up some omelets, topped them with beluga caviar, and were thankful that we did not have to eat sweet potatoes with melted marshmallows.

This Thanksgiving proved a challenge. A few detective colleagues generously and sincerely invited me to join them. No, that wasn't for me. So I volunteered for holiday assignment. But

Inspector Elliott informed me that Thanksgiving was well-staffed with both detectives and officers (mostly divorced parents who traded seeing their children on Thanksgiving Day for seeing them on Christmas Day).

For a moment I wondered how my partner would be spending her holiday. Although my knowledge of K. Burke's private life was sparse, I knew that both her parents were deceased.

Casually I asked her, "Where are you going for Thanksgiving?"

"The gym," was her answer.

In an unlikely explosion of sentiment that surprised even myself I said, "Come to my place. I'll fix Thanksgiving dinner for both of us."

"Yeah, sure," was her sarcastic reaction. "And I'll bake a pumpkin pie."

"No. I'm serious."

"You are?" she said, trying to hide her surprise.

With only a hint of confusion she spoke slowly and quietly. "Oh, my God. This feels like a date."

"I assure you, it is not," I said.

Both Burke and I knew that I meant it.

Then I added, "But please do *not* bake a pumpkin pie."

CHAPTER 2

Thanksgiving

"THIS PLACE IS… well, it's sort of unbelievable," K. Burke says. She stands in the entrance gallery to my new apartment and spreads her arms in amazement.

"Merci," I say. "I had to find a new home after Dalia died. I could not stay in her place. I could not stay in mine. Too many…" I pause.

Detective Burke nods. Of course, she knows. Too many memories. I take her on a brief tour of the place. A loft on Madison Square, a single three-thousand-foot room with a view of the Flatiron Building to the south and the Empire State Building to the north. The huge room is sparse—purposely so. Steel furniture, glass side tables, black-and-white Cartier-Bresson photographs of Paris.

We eventually move to the table for Thanksgiving dinner. The small black lacquered table is set with my great-grandmother's vintage Limoges.

As we begin the main course of the dinner, K. Burke says, "The only thing more impressive than this apartment is this meal."

Another *Merci*.

"Moncrief, I've known you almost a year. I've spent hundreds of hours with you. I've been on a police case in Europe with you. I…I never knew you could cook like this. I just can't believe you can make a meal like this."

"Well, K. Burke. I *cannot* make a meal like this. But fortunately Steve Miller, the senior sous-chef at Gramercy Tavern, was happy to make such a meal."

And what a feast it is.

Burke and I begin with a truffled chestnut soup. Then, instead of a big bird plopped in the middle of the table, Miller has layered thin slices of turkey breast in a creamy sauce of Gruyère cheese and porcini mushrooms. Instead of the dreaded sweet potatoes, we are dining on crisp pommes frites and a delicious cool salad, a combination of shredded brussels sprouts and pomegranate seeds.

"This is what the food in heaven tastes like," K. Burke says.

"No, this is what the food in Gramercy Tavern tastes like."

I pour us each some wine. We clink glasses.

"What shall we toast to?" she says.

I say, "Let us toast to a good friendship during a difficult year."

She hesitates just for a moment. Then K. Burke says, "Yes. To a good friendship."

We drink.

She holds up her glass again.

"One more thing I want to toast to," Burke says.

"Yes?" I say, hoping it will not be sentimental, hoping it will not be about Dalia, hoping…

"Let's toast to you and me really trying to see eye to eye from now on."

"Excellent idea," I say. We clink glasses again. We begin to devour the wonderful food.

And then her cell phone rings. Burke quickly puts down her fork and slips the phone out of her pocket. She reads the name.

"It's Inspector Elliott."

"Don't answer it," I say.

"We've got to answer it, Moncrief."

"Don't answer it," I repeat. "*We* are having dinner."

"*You* are a lunatic," she says.

I roll my eyes and speak.

"So much for trying to see eye to eye."

CHAPTER 3

OF COURSE, K. BURKE triumphs. She takes Inspector Elliott's call.

Fifteen minutes later we're in the detective squad room of Midtown East watching Elliott eat a slice of pie. K. Burke later tells me that it is filled with something called mincemeat, made out of beef fat and brandy. *Incroyable!*

"This could have waited until tomorrow, but you both told me that you wanted to work today. So I assumed you'd be free," Elliott says.

Then he looks us both up and down closely, Burke in a simple, elegant gray skirt with a black shirt; me in a navy blue Brioni bespoke suit.

"But you both are dressed like you've just come from the White House."

Neither Burke nor I speak. We are certainly not going to tell our boss where we were dining fifteen minutes earlier.

"In any event, I decided to come in and do some desk work. My wife packed me some pie. And I figured I could watch Green Bay kick the Bears' ass on my iPad instead of watching it on TV with my brother-in-law."

Then he gets down to business.

"I thought this problem might go away, but it's real. Very real. Potentially dangerous. And it involves some New York City big shots."

Elliott swallows the last chunk of his pie. Then he continues speaking. He's energetic, anxious. Whatever it is, it's going to be a big deal.

"You two ever heard of the Namanworth Gallery up on 57th Street?"

"I think so," says Burke. "Just off Park Avenue."

"That's the one," says Elliott. "You know the place, Moncrief? It sounds like something you'd be down with."

"As a matter of fact, I *do* know that gallery. They handled the sale of a Kandinsky to a friend of mine a few months ago, and a few years back my father was talking to them about a Rothko. Nothing came of it."

"Well, your dad might have lucked out," says Elliott. "We've got some pretty heavy evidence that they've been dealing in the most impeccable forgeries in New York. A lot of collectors have been screwed over by them."

I speak.

"Namanworth hasn't owned that place for thirty years. A husband and wife are the owners. Sophia and Andre Krane. I think she claims to have been a countess or duchess or something."

"We don't know about her royal blood. But we do know that Barney Wexler, the guy who owns that cosmetics company, paid them thirty-five million dollars for a Klimt painting. And he thinks it was…"

I finish his sentence for him. "…not painted by Klimt."

Elliott says, "And Wexler's lined up two experts who can back him up."

"Although the case sounds really exciting…" Burke says, "there's a special division for art-and-antique counterfeit work."

"Yeah," says Elliott. "But with these big players, there may be more to it than simple forgery. Where there's smoke, there's usually fire. And where there's valuable artwork, there's possible fraud, possible money-laundering—ultimately, possible homicides. So they want us to stick our dirty noses in it. We can call on counterfeit if we want."

I speak. "I don't think we'll want to do that."

"That's what I thought you'd say, Moncrief." Then he taps a button on his computer. "There, I've just sent you all the info on the case. You'll see. It's not just Wexler. These are the money-men *and* the money-women who rock this town.

"By the way, there's a special pain in the ass about this case.…"

"Isn't there always?" Burke says.

"This is particularly painful," says Elliott. "The Kranes aren't talking. They're comfy in their eight-hundred-acre Catskills estate."

"The hell with that," says Burke. "We'll get an order from justice."

"No, you won't, not when the attorney general of the state of New York says they don't have to cooperate."

"What the hell is that all about?" I say.

"Exactly," says Elliott. "What the hell is that all about?"

He lets out a long breath of air and swivels to face his PC.

As we walk away from Elliott's desk, K. Burke lays out her plan to download all information on the Namanworth Gallery, all information on Barney Wexler, all information on Sophia and Andre Krane, and all classified insurance information on important international collectors.

"What's your plan, Moncrief?" she asks.

"First, I think we should return to my home and finish our dinner."

"And then?" she asks.

"And then I'll call my friends who collect art."

CHAPTER 4

K. BURKE LIKES to do things by the book. I like to do things by the gut. This is our professional relationship. This is also our ongoing problem.

"It looks like we'll be spending the day at this desk, Moncrief," she says. Do I detect a note of smug satisfaction in her voice?

But of course I do.

Black Friday, the day after Thanksgiving. Almost everyone will be open for what America calls door-busting sales, but the truly fashionable establishments—certainly the 57th Street galleries—will be locked up tight. No wealthy collector is going to be shopping for a Jasper Johns today.

"I have been at this desk for thirty minutes, and I've accomplished nothing," I say to Detective Burke.

"Try turning the computer *on,*" Burke says.

I stand and inform her that I'll be doing a little "on-the-street wandering." Burke simply shakes her head and smiles. She knows by now that both of us will be better off if I'm out doing "my kind of police work."

Twenty minutes later I am entering a shop at the corner of Lexington Avenue and 63rd Street, J. Pocker, the finest art framer in New York City.

"I think you may have used us before," says the very gracious (and very pretty) Asian woman who greets me.

"Yes," I say. "A few years ago. You framed two photographs for me."

"Yes, you're the Frenchman. You brought in those Dorothea Lange portraits. Depressing, but very beautiful," she says.

"Isn't that sometimes the way?" I ask. I feel myself shifting into Automatic Flirt.

I look through the glass partition behind the huge measuring table at the rear of the shop. Two bearded young men are working with wood and glass and metal wire.

"So, how may I help you today, sir?" the woman says.

I pull out my personal cell phone. A photograph of a painting by Gary Kuehn comes up. It is essentially a pencil, ink, and oil drawing of a slice of the moon. The moon is a deep dark blue. It hangs against an equally dark gray-brown sky. It is beautiful, and it hung in the bedroom that Dalia and I once shared.

"I need to have this piece reframed. The frame is a cheap black thing. I had it done in Germany some time ago, when I bought the piece."

"It's a Kuehn," she says. "I like his work."

She walks to the measuring table and pulls out a sample of maple and one of thin shiny steel.

"I think either of these would be worth considering. I prefer simple subject matter to have a corresponding simple frame. I know that the French prefer contrast—a Klee inside an ornate Renaissance-type frame, but consider…"

I cut her off. "The Frenchman agrees with your suggestion."

"Please take the samples with you. You can return them after you've made your choice."

I thank her, and as I am about to leave she says, "I've seen a lot of Kuehn's work lately. He's older. But he's become very popular recently."

"As a fan of his, I must ask, how much of his work have you seen recently?"

"Certainly three or four canvases," she says. "Many of them—I think—are similar to the one you own. Curves. Circles. A sort of defiance of space."

Ah, the babble and bullshit of the art world.

"Yes," I repeat. "A defiance of space."

She smiles.

I tell her that I will be back. Yes. I will definitely be back.

CHAPTER 5

I WATCH THE SHOPPERS. Today's shopping could be classified as a sort of athletic event. People barely able to carry their exploding shopping bags. Huge flat-screen television sets lugged by happy men. Packs of happy people, angry people, exhausted people.

I have seen the videos of women punching one another to snatch the last green Shetland sweater at H&M. Entire families—mothers, fathers, wailing children—waiting outside Macy's since four in the morning so they can be the first to race down the aisles.

I take in all the madness as I walk the six blocks down and one avenue over from 63rd Street to 57th Street. I turn right. Yes, Namanworth Gallery will be shut tight, but I am so close that I must visit.

An ornate carved steel door covers the entrance. The one front window holds a single easel that holds a single large impressionist canvas. It is famous. A painting by Monet. The painting is framed with baroque gold-leaf wood. It is one painting in Monet's series of haystacks.

The subtle beauty of color and craft eludes me. I cannot help myself. I examine it purely as a possible forgery.

I pull up the series of paintings on my phone and quickly find the one I'm looking at. I know I am on a fool's errand. The tiny phone photo and the gorgeous real painting cannot be compared. Is a straw out of place? Is *that* smudge of cloud identical to *that* smudge of cloud?

Wait. What about the artist's signature?

I recently read that a woman had a Jackson Pollock painting hanging in her entrance hall for twenty years. No one—not the woman, not her guests—ever noticed that the artist's signature was spelled incorrectly: "Pollack" instead of "Pollock."

No such luck. A big bold signature: Claude Monet. Not Manet. Not Maret.

"Monet" is "Monet." How could I expect to be so lucky?

I decide to take a few photographs of the painting. I am not sure why I need photographs, but they might somehow someday come in handy. I move to the left, then right. I try to avoid the glare on the window.

Now I hear a voice from behind me. "You taking a picture for the folks back home?"

Mon Dieu! I have been mistaken for a tourist.

I turn and see a portly middle-aged man. He is wearing an inexpensive gray suit with an inexpensive gray tie. He wears a heavy raincoat and a brown fedora. He is smoking a cigarette.

"Beautiful painting," the man says.

"It certainly is," I say, as I slip my phone into my suit jacket.

"I'm one of the security people for Namanworth's," the man says. "You've been looking at that picture for quite a while."

There is no threat in his voice, no anger.

"I have a great interest in Monet," I say. "The Haystacks series in particular."

"Apparently a lot of people have an interest in this stuff," the man says. "I work out of that second floor front office. Just me and my binoculars."

He gestures in the direction of the elegant stationery store across the street. It is the same store where I have my business cards engraved.

"I just thought I'd come ask what's so intriguing about that painting. It seems to have caught a lot of attention today. Not just the usual shoppers and tourists," he says.

"Well, who else, then?" I ask as casually as I can.

"Well, there was a man and a woman, a young couple. They were driving a Bentley. Double-parked it. Then they began shooting their iPhones at the painting. Little later two guys in one of those Mercedes SUVs jumped out; these guys had big fancy cameras, real professional-looking. Then I saw you...and anyway, I needed a smoke."

"And do you have any idea what the others wanted?" I ask.

"Just art lovers, I guess. Anyway, they looked kinda rich. Sorta like you—now that I see you close-up. I guess you're too fancy to be a tourist."

A twinge of relief. Then the security man flicks his cigarette onto 57th Street.

"Did you record the license numbers of the cars?" I ask.

"No. They weren't doing anything *that* unusual. Could be they were thinking of buying it. I'm just here to make sure nobody breaks the window…though it's as unbreakable as you can get."

"I'm sure it is," I say.

"Well, you have a good day," the man says. He walks to the curb, looks both ways. He turns back toward me and speaks.

"You're French, right?"

"I am, yes."

"I thought so."

I am so obviously French that I might as well have a statue of the Eiffel Tower on my head. But the man is pleased with his detective work. Then he crosses the street.

I take a final look at the Monet.

I am about to make my way to Madison Avenue when, without warning, I think about Dalia. I freeze in place. People walk around me, past me.

Suddenly I am overwhelmed by sadness. It is not depression. It is not physical. It is…well, it is a sort of disease of the heart. It always comes without warning. It is always dreadful, painful.

Fortunately, I know just what to do.

CHAPTER 6

SHOPPING IS THE ANSWER. For me it is almost always the answer. So I join the holiday madness. An uncontrolled shopping spree, for some unfathomable reason, always brings me peace.

My mind clicks madly away as to how I can best visit the many extraordinary stores on 57th Street.

Like a recovering alcoholic who studiously avoids bars, I almost always avoid this area. The merchandise is so tempting, so upscale, so expensive.

Where to start? That's so easy. The Namanworth Gallery is a block away from Robinson Antiques. Surprisingly, it's open. This shop is only for the wealthy cognoscenti of New York—eighteenth-century silver sugar shakers, Sheffield candelabras that hold twelve candles, a rare oil painting of a cocker spaniel or a hunting dog, another of a Thoroughbred at Ascot. A mahogany wig stand, one whose provenance says that it was one of twenty that once stood in the Houses of Parliament. The distinguished-looking old salesman says, "May I help you?" Five minutes later I have become the proud owner of four sterling silver Georgian marrow scoops. $7,300.

The salesman wants to explain the insignia of King George III on the reverse side of the scoops. I tell him to please hurry. "I have to be someplace."

The place "I have to be" is also nearby—Niketown. One of the first things K. Burke said when we began working together was, "You are the only person I've ever met who can find sneakers that look as if they were made by a Renaissance artist."

Burke was right. The sneakers she had seen were black high-tops with a small brass clasp, Nike by Giuseppe Zanotti. Today the store manager escorts me to "The Vault," a small room in the back of the very busy store. When I leave the Vault I am wearing a pair of black Ferragamo Nikes—black with thin white soles, the distinctive Gancini buckle. As I exit Niketown I think, *"I must be insane. Except to play an occasional game of squash, I never wear sneakers."* This thought, however, lasts only for a minute. By then I am back across 57th Street at Louis Vuitton where I'm examining an oversized overnight bag. It is made with simple soft brown leather. It does not have the ostentatious LV pattern on it. It is beautiful. It is perfect. Not at all like my life.

Now I am only a few yards from the Van Cleef & Arpels entrance at Bergdorf Goodman. I can do some real damage here.

The Van Cleef doorman is still holding the door open when my phone buzzes. The red light. Burke.

"Your day's just beginning, Moncrief," she says.

"What's going on?"

"I see you're at 57th and Fifth."

"Right," I say.

"Get over to 61st and Park, number 535. Somebody decided to

murder the elderly Mrs. Ramona Driver Dunlop. Or as they still call her on the gossip blogs, Baby D."

"Ramona Dunlop?" I say. "I didn't know she was still alive."

"She's not," Burke says.

"Good one, Detective. Very good."

CHAPTER 7

I EXPECT THE usual homicide pandemonium. But this is over-the-top madness. Twice the sirens, twice the flashing lights, twice the news reporters. I should not be surprised.

After all, this was Baby D. In 1944 she was Debutante of the Year. In 1946 she married Ray Dunlop, a Philadelphia millionaire who had inherited extremely valuable patents on ballpoint pens and mechanical pencils. In 1948 she divorced Dunlop and took up with a waiter from the Stork Club.

The lobby of 535 Park is cluttered with the usual detectives and forensic folks. An NYPD detective holds up four fingers. Then he nods toward the elevator. An elevator man takes me up to the fourth floor. The elevator doors open directly into the foyer of the Dunlop apartment. K. Burke is standing with four senior officers. She waves at me, and then approaches.

"You waved?" I say. "Did you think I wouldn't be able to find you in that ocean of blue?"

Burke ignores my comment, glances at my shopping bags and says, "Little man, you've had a busy day."

"In a manner of speaking, yes," I say.

"Follow me," she says. Burke and I turn right and walk down a long narrow hallway.

These hall walls are cluttered with photos and paintings and framed documents: an invitation to President Kennedy's inauguration; a cover of LIFE magazine that verifies Baby D as "New York's Debutante of the Year." Then I see a large Lichtenstein cartoon panel. It hangs next to a much smaller Hockney diving board and swimming pool. I linger for a moment and take in the paintings.

Then we are in Mrs. Dunlop's bedroom. Also in the bedroom are Nick Elliott and assistant ME, Dr. Rosita Guittierez.

"Where's Nicole Reeves?" I ask. Elliott understands, of course, that I am referring to the fact that Guittierez is an *assistant,* while Reeves is the big boss.

"She must be out shopping," Elliott says.

"Like everyone else," Burke adds.

The late Mrs. Ramona Driver Dunlop is resting, very dead, in her king-sized bed with the powder-blue satin-covered headboard. Mrs. Dunlop is covered with protective plastic police cloth, from her shoulders down to and including her feet. What's left exposed is the dry bloody slash that begins at the jawbone below one ear and extends the entire width of the neck to the other ear. The face is thin and, as with many women of a certain age, has the high-puffed chipmunk-like cheeks that only a significant facelift can guarantee.

Burke asks Elliott for the details. Elliott hands the floor over to Rosita Guittierez.

"Looks like we're talking about six o' clock this morning when this happened. Sharp-bladed instrument, probably a knife. You can see the wound is U-shaped. So it got all the jugulars—internal, external, posterior. It got the carotids. She partially bled out. No sign of force. They got the old girl while she was still asleep."

Burke listens carefully. I pretend to listen, but I am more interested in looking around the room—light-blue walls matching the satin on the headboard, an ornate crystal chandelier more appropriate for a ballroom, mock Provincial side tables, and bureaus with random dabs of white and gray paint to give a distressed antique look. And one odd detail: Except for a full-length mirror behind the bathroom door, nothing is hanging on the walls. Absolutely nothing.

CHAPTER 8

WE LEARN WHAT little else is left to learn.

Mrs. Dunlop spent most of Thanksgiving Day at her son and daughter-in-law's house in Bedford. The only other person who was in the apartment after her return was a maid. The maid discovered the victim at the time she always woke Mrs. Dunlop.

Three medical staff police now pack up Mrs. Dunlop and wheel her out.

Elliott speaks.

"What do you guys think?"

"My guess is that it's a burglary gone bad," says Burke. "Holiday weekend. Lots of places empty. The intruder could have had inside information. What do you think, Moncrief?"

"Perhaps," I say. "Always perhaps. I see nothing to prove otherwise, but I also see nothing to support the theory. So for the time being, let's embrace Detective Burke's theory."

Elliott nods and says—as only an American detective can say easily and without irony—"I'll see you guys back at the morgue."

He leaves, and K. Burke speaks. "Thanks for supporting my theory. I wasn't really expecting that."

I smile. "Don't get used to it, K. Burke. I am not so concerned with this murder as I am concerned with the circumstances *surrounding* this murder."

"And that means?" says Burke.

"The victim was almost ninety years old. May God bless her and welcome her into His paradise. Baby D has lived a life of enormous pleasure and wealth. *But…* fresh off our investigation of the Namanworth Gallery…*I notice something interesting.* Hanging outside her bedroom are paintings by Lichtenstein and Hockney. Only they are forgeries. The small dots in the 'talk bubbles' on the Lichtenstein are too neatly spaced to be authentic. And the swimming pool in the Hockney should be more rectangular."

Burke says exactly what I am expecting her to say.

"You can't be the first person to have noticed that."

"Perhaps. Perhaps not. But I don't think that too many art connoisseurs traverse that hallway. The possibility may also exist that Baby D knew that her pieces were forgeries and it made little difference to her. Like a print of the *Mona Lisa* in a small apartment in Clichy. It brings the owners joy. Perhaps the same was true with Madame Dunlop and her modern masterpieces."

"We need to tell Elliott about this," Burke says.

"I don't want him breathing down our necks. At least not yet. We will return tomorrow morning, let the others finish the interviews. We'll have more information and more space to examine the apartment closely, see what we can see, find what we can find."

"This is not going to end well, Moncrief. I don't like doing things this way."

"I know you don't," I say. "That's what makes it such an adventure."

CHAPTER 9

THERE ARE ONLY three things in this world that I truly hate: over-cooked vegetables, flannel sheets, and whenever K. Burke is right about something.

This next day is one of those times.

We arrive at 535 Park Avenue at 8:00 a.m. There is still a "modified police presence"—one NYPD officer at the corner of Park and 61st Street, a second officer in the small mailroom, a plain-clothesman in the lobby. It's the usual set-up for a post-homicide scene.

Burke and I bring with us two big evidence cases marked "NYPD." These will be used to carry the forged Lichtenstein and Hockney. When the elevator opens at the Dunlop apartment we exchange hellos with Ralph Ortiz, a smart up-and-coming rookie who's stuck guarding the crime scene.

"Allons-y," I say. "Let's go."

"I know what *allons* means, Moncrief," she says. "I've only told you a few thousand times. You do *not* have to translate for me. I know French. That's one of the reasons they teamed us up."

"Ah, oui," I say. Then I say, "That means 'yes.'"

Burke ignores me as we walk toward the hallway.

And then…son of a bitch! The paintings are missing.

Softly Burke says, "Goddamnit."

I turn quickly and rush down the hallway to Officer Ortiz.

"How long have you been on duty?"

"Since midnight," he says. Ortiz senses that something's not right. He immediately answers the question I would have asked.

"Nobody's been in or out. Nobody. Not a soul," he says. And then, because he's as sharp as any kid I know in the NYPD, he says, "And I never heard anyone. I never saw anyone. I checked on the master bedroom and the other rooms every hour. I know…"

"Okay, okay," I say. "I'm sure nothing got by you."

"Only something *did* get by him," Burke says. "A bunch of officers and detectives on surveillance and two paintings disappear."

"Listen, these things happen. These things…" But she cuts me off.

"Goddamnit," says Burke. "I should never have listened to you. We should have gotten the info to Elliott and *then* together the three of us could proceed. But you. You have your own ways. The goddamn *instinct*."

My anger about the paintings, along with Burke's rant, now makes me explode.

"Yes. And my ways are good ways, smart ways. History proves it. My ways usually work!"

Burke shakes her head and talks in a calm, normal voice.

"The operative word here is 'usually.' I'm going back to the precinct house."

"I'll join you shortly," I say. We are quiet.

I know this brief two-sentence conversation is as close as Burke and I will come to signing a peace treaty.

As soon as K. Burke leaves, Ortiz and I check the apartment, walking the rooms for any detail that might stand out. Nothing. Pantry. Maid's rooms. Butler's pantry. Service hall. *Nothing.* Silver closet. China closet. Powder rooms. *Nothing.* Dressing rooms. Kitchen (and impressive wine collection). Office. Dining room. *Nothing. Nothing. Nothing.*

I rush back to the hallway wall where the Lichtenstein and Hockney once hung. I study the two empty spaces of the wall— as if the paintings might magically have reappeared, as if I could magically "wish" them back to the wall.

Finally, I say to Ortiz, "I cannot stay in this apartment any longer. If I do, I will explode like a human bomb."

CHAPTER 10

IT IS BARELY ELEVEN in the morning when I leave Baby D's apartment. The day is cold and crisp, and to the happy person… Christmas is in the air. The sadness that I've come to know so well begins to descend. As the doctors say, "Rate your pain on a scale of one to ten, ten being the most painful." I would call it a six or seven.

I walk down Park Avenue and turn left on 59th Street. I am at a store I enjoy enormously, Argosy, the home of rare maps and prints, antiquarian books. Perhaps a $30,000 volume of hand-colored Audubon birds will lift my spirits. Perhaps a letter addressed to John Adams and signed by Benjamin Franklin will cheer me up. I touch the soft leather on the binding of a first-edition *Madame Bovary*. I study a fifteenth-century map of my native land—a survey of France so misshapen and inaccurate, it might as well be a picture of a dead fish. But I buy nothing.

The same happens to me in Pesca, a swimsuit shop, where Dalia once bought a pale-yellow bikini for five hundred dollars, where I could buy an old-fashioned pair of trunks with a bronze buckle in front for $550 and look just like *mon grand-père* on the beach in Deauville. I move on to other shops.

But nothing is for me. Not the art deco silver ashtrays, not the leather iPad cases that cost more than the iPads that they hold.

No. Not for me. But also not for me are the street corner Santa Clauses, the exquisite twinkling white lights in the windows of the townhouses, the impromptu Christmas tree lots on Third Avenue.

In the season of buying I have, for once, bought nothing.

CHAPTER 11

I REALLY DO intend to return to Midtown East and meet with K. Burke. Really. But then other instincts take over. I decide to return to 535 Park Avenue. I must make a dent in this case. I must redeem myself.

I walk back toward Baby D's building. This morning I interviewed the super, a handsome middle-aged guy named Ed Petrillo. Like most Park Avenue supers Petrillo wears a suit, has an office, and thinks he's running a business like General Motors or Microsoft. He says he was at his weekend house (the super has a weekend house!) for Thanksgiving.

I also spoke with the first-shift doorman, Jing-Ho. He was not aware of anything unusual. He suggested that I talk to George, the doorman who came on after him. I let other detectives speak to George, but now I need to stick my own fingers into this pie.

I arrive at the building and exchange a few words with the police guard at the corner of Park and 61st. "Nothing suspicious, nothing extraordinary." He's seen a bunch of limos outside the Regency Hotel across the street. He's seen a celebrity—either Taylor Swift *or* Carrie Underwood. He's not sure. (Hell, even I would know the difference.)

George the Doorman has the full name of George Brooks. The dark-blue uniform with gold braid fits him well. He wears black leather gloves.

"In winter we wear leather gloves. Other times of the year it's strictly white gloves. White gloves are what separates the 'good' buildings from the 'cheesy' buildings."

He is a polite guy, maybe thirty-five.

"Listen, Detective, not to be uncooperative or anything, but two other detectives have already asked me a bunch of questions—all I can do is tell you what I told them. I really don't know much. I mean, Mrs. Dunlop didn't have many guests. Just the usual deliveries through the service entrance—groceries, flowers, Amazon, liquor."

"Just tell me anything unusual about the day she died," I say. "Even if you think it's not important, just tell me."

"Nothing. Really nothing. She had come back Thursday night from the country. Her regular driver dropped her off." He pauses for a moment. "I didn't like the driver, but who the hell cares about what I think."

"I care quite a bit about what you think. Why didn't you like him?"

"He wasn't here long, but he thought he was better than the building staff. Because he drove a rich lady around in a car. A big black Caddy, an Escalade. Who gives a shit? Here's a good example: drivers are not supposed to wait in the lobby. That's the rule. They either stay in the car or go downstairs to the locker room. The driver was always standing outside smoking or sitting on the bench right here by the intercom phone. So I tell Mr. Petrillo about it…"

"The super," I say.

"The super, yeah. So Mr. P. tells him he can't do it anymore, and Simon says that that's bullshit. He says he's going to tell Mrs. Dunlop. Mr. Petrillo says go right ahead. Well, I guess Mrs. Dunlop agrees with the rules of the building. So the next thing you know—*bam!*—Mrs. Dunlop is getting a new driver."

I've read all this previously, in the interviews taken down by the other detectives, but I do notice a small trace of triumph in George Brooks's face when he arrives at the climax of his story.

I also know that the driver, whose full name is the very impressive moniker "Preston Parker Simon," did *not* say he was fired. According to his manager, he'd quit. K. Burke had checked Simon out with Domestic Bliss, an employment agency that places maids, laundresses, chauffeurs, and the occasional butler. Simon hadn't answered her calls, but a manager at Domestic Bliss, Miss Devida Pickering, told Burke that Simon was honest and dependable. But, she said, Mrs. Dunlop only used him part-time, and Simon wanted to be a full-time chauffeur. So that was that. But as that is never *really* that, we would need to track him down. He was the last person to see Baby D alive. I thank George. He offers me his hand to shake. I, of course, shake it.

I tell him thank you.

He says, "It's been great talking with you, absolutely great."

CHAPTER 12

A MINUTE LATER, I am in the basement of the building. My interviewee is fifty-four years old and is wearing khaki pants with a matching shirt. The shirt has the words "535 Park" emblazoned in red thread on the pocket.

The man's name is Angel Corrido, and Angel stands in the doorway of the service elevator. As we talk he removes clear plastic bags of very classy recycling. Along with the newspapers and Q-tips boxes are empty bottles of excellent Bordeaux and Johnnie Walker Black Label, empty take-out containers from Café Boulud.

I've already been briefed on his initial interviews on the scene, so my first question is the old standby: "Could you tell me anything I might not know about Mrs. Dunlop?"

He shrugs, then speaks. "No, nothing. Mrs. Dunlop never sees Angel Corrido."

"Never?"

"Eh, maybe sometimes." He removes a bundled stack of magazines.

"When I see her…Mrs. Dunlop…she is nice. She says, 'Hello, Angel. How are the wife and the children?'"

Angel laughs and says, "I have stopped telling her that I don't have a wife and I don't have children. She don't remember. She is nice, but a man who runs the back elevator blends in with the other men who run back elevators and shovel snow and take out garbage."

Angel does not sound angry at this. He actually seems to think it's amusing.

"Were you working here on Thanksgiving?" I ask.

"No, I come to work early the next morning. No back elevator on Thanksgiving."

He takes the last bag of recycling from the elevator. Then he throws a glance at the stairs leading down from the lobby above.

"But Angel *can* tell you something you do not know. But it is not about Mrs. Dunlop. It is about someone else."

"Yeah?"

He says nothing.

"So what is it?"

Still silence.

Then I do what no NYPD detective is ever supposed to do. I take a fifty-dollar bill from my pocket and hand it to him.

"So?"

"So maybe you should know something about that big-shot *el cabrón* who holds the door open for people, George Brooks," says Angel.

"Go on," I say.

"You know the way you just tipped me?"

"Yeah."

"That is the way the *chofer* for Mrs. Dunlop used to tip George every week. One hundred dollars when he delivers Mrs. Dunlop the big packages from the art gallery."

"The Namanworth Gallery?" I ask.

Angel speaks.

"Yes, maybe that is the name. I am not always good when I try to remember names. You know, when you are not born in this country—it is sometimes hard."

"Yes," I say. "It is sometimes *very* hard."

I thank him. I run up the stairs.

I text K. Burke: Need more info on driver P Simon. Let's find him.

CHAPTER 13

BURKE TELEPHONES DOMESTIC BLISS again. They have no current address for Preston Parker Simon, but she finds out that he is now driving for the CEO of a large and very successful comedy video website.

Making up for their failure to maintain addresses for their employees, Domestic Bliss does have the capability to track their drivers while they're driving clients. In a few minutes Burke finds out that the Escalade, presumably with Preston Parker Simon in the driver's seat, is parked outside the Four Seasons Hotel.

All roads in this case seem to lead to 57th Street. The Four Seasons is neatly bookended with Brioni, the men's fashion hot spot, on one side and Zilli, the French luxury brand, on the other side.

Burke and I meet up outside the hotel. A parade of limos, SUVs, and two Bentleys are waiting there. Their engines are running, poised to whisk away some business tycoon or rap star or foreign princess.

Burke punches some buttons on her phone, and soon we're asking Simon to step out of the Escalade.

He turns out to be a good-looking blond guy, certainly no older than thirty. He's charming, cooperative, and he has a fancy British accent that fits perfectly with his fancy British name.

Burke tells him that we're investigating the murder of Mrs. Ramona Dunlop. As soon as we do, a look of horror crosses his face.

"I heard. I saw it on the telly yesterday. Quite horrid. You know, I worked briefly for Mrs. Dunlop."

"Up until yesterday, you were her chauffeur," Burke says.

"Lovely woman. Remarkably spry for her age," Simon says.

He pulls out a tortoiseshell cigarette case from his jacket and offers us a cigarette.

"Have a fag?" he asks. Then he adds, "I love saying that to Americans. Always good for a laugh."

Burke and I decline the cigarette. We also decline to laugh.

"How long did you work for Mrs. Dunlop?" Burke asks.

"Not more than a month. She had a home in East Hampton. So a few times I took her out there. But she only really needed me for an occasional trip to the Colony Club for lunch, sometimes the opera, once or twice to her son's house in Bedford. It was not working out financially for me. I sought other clients."

"You drove her up to her son's house Thanksgiving Day, correct?" I ask.

"Quite correct."

"Though you had already given your notice?"

"Yes. She had hired a new driver, but we agreed I'd work through the holiday."

"How long were you and Mrs. Dunlop up there?" I ask.

"About four hours. We left for the city around six o'clock. I think I had her back on her doorstep by seven fifteen, maybe seven thirty."

Burke says, "Did you help her into the building with her things?"

"Things?" Simon asks, confused.

"Yeah," says Burke. "Things. Luggage. Packages. Leftover stuffing."

"Oh, no, no, no. There was a doorman. Very posh place. Lovely mansion," says Simon.

"535 Park Avenue is an apartment building, a co-op," says Burke.

I speak. "In England an apartment building sometimes is called 'a mansion.'"

"Live and learn, I guess," says Burke.

When did he officially resign from his job with Mrs. Dunlop? Yesterday.

Has he had reason to return to 535 Park since her death? No.

Who's he working for now?

"Danny Abosch, a dot-com prince," he says. "Lovely young chap."

As if on cue, a guy who looks like a college student who's late for class exits the hotel.

"Mr. Abosch is approaching," says Simon. "I really have to dash."

K. Burke responds to a crackle from her radio. I tell Simon that we may want to talk to him again. He says, "Surely," but his attention is on his boss, the young man in a blue Shetland sweater and a red ski parka walking toward us.

As Preston Parker Simon moves to open the car door he hands me a "calling card"—name, number, email. Engraved. Beige paper. Garamond type.

A chauffeur with his own calling card.

And they say I'm fancy.

CHAPTER 14

K. BURKE AND I begin walking from the Four Seasons Hotel down Fifth Avenue. We're headed back to police headquarters on East 51st Street.

A few minutes pass in silence. Then I speak.

"Preston Parker Simon is not an Englishman," I say.

"He sure does a good imitation of one," K. Burke says.

"Precisely," I answer. "His accent is purely *theatrical*. It is not authentic. In England someone from Yorkshire sounds distinctly different from someone from Cornwall. *Monsieur le chauffeur* has an all-purpose stage accent, the kind Gwyneth Paltrow uses in the cinema."

"You're good, Moncrief," Burke says. "Very good."

"Merci," I say.

"But you aren't telling me anything I don't already know."

"You could detect it also?" I ask.

"No. Simon might as well have been Prince Charles as far as I could tell."

We stop to look at the Christmas display in the windows of Bergdorf Goodman. It is sparkly and sexy and crazy. Neptune and half-dressed female statues and the Baby Jesus. Toward the back of all this opulence is a crystal Eiffel Tower—homage to the horror of the hideous Paris terrorist attacks. I turn away.

"So, go on," I say to Burke. She speaks.

"While we were finishing up with Simon I received a 'birth and background' file from downtown. They found out that Preston Parker Simon's real name is Rudy Brunetti. He's from Morristown, New Jersey. He was born and raised there, and then…"

"And then he became an actor," I venture.

"Don't try to speed ahead of me, Moncrief."

"Forgive my enthusiasm," I say.

"*Then* Simon went to Lincoln Technical Institute. That's in Edison, New Jersey. *Then* he became a karate instructor. *Then* he became an actor."

"And after that he became a chauffeur," I say.

"What did I tell you about speeding ahead of me? No."

She takes out her iPad and consults it for the rest of Simon's bio.

"Then he signed up with Domestic Bliss. He got a job as a personal assistant to one of Ralph Lauren's designers. Then for a year he was a butler at the French consulate.…"

"And he fooled the French?" I exclaim as if I were shocked. *"Mon Dieu!"*

"*Then* he became a driver. First to Mrs. Dunlop. Now to this Abosch kid at the comedy website. By the way, neither the police nor Domestic Bliss has an address for him, just a post office box in Grand Central."

Burke and I are about to turn onto 51st Street. We pause to

admire the huge wreath on the front of St. Patrick's Cathedral. It is lighted with thousands of lights.

Then I lose interest in the wreath. My mind still lingers on the window of Bergdorf Goodman—the crystal *Tour Eiffel* a few blocks away, the wrought-iron *Tour Eiffel* a few thousand miles away.

I should be used to Burke's amazing sensitivity, but this time I am truly astonished.

"You're thinking of the Paris attacks, aren't you, Moncrief?" she says.

"You are a very wise woman, K. Burke."

"My heart breaks for you and your countrymen."

I nod. Then I say, "I know. I know it does. But enough gloom for now. Tell me. What do you think the next steps should be with Rudy Brunetti?"

"Let's go pick him up and find out what the story is, yes?"

I speak slowly, thoughtfully.

"No. I have another idea. Let us wait a few hours. My plan may turn out to be more helpful."

CHAPTER 15

NINE O'CLOCK THAT EVENING.

Burke and I sit in a car on Tenth Avenue and 20th Street in the shadow of Manhattan's newest beloved tourist attraction, the High Line.

I had wanted to drive my 1962 light-blue Corvette for this job. K. Burke's reaction to that idea?

"Forget it, Moncrief. You might as well have a brass band marching in front of that Corvette. They designed that car to attract attention," she said. Grudgingly, I told her she was correct.

So we sit in an unmarked NYPD patrol car. A Honda? A Chevy? Who cares? We are watching Preston Parker Simon who is sitting in his black Escalade outside a brand-new thirty-five-story building. The three of us are waiting for the same thing—the young internet video tycoon. Once Simon picks up the "rich kid" we will tail them. Domestic Bliss can only track him when he's on the clock; our objective is to discover the location of the place that Simon calls home.

Fifteen minutes later we see Simon get out of his SUV. He holds the door open for Danny Abosch. They exchange what appear to be some pleasant words. The kid steps inside the car. They take off.

Simon's car turns right onto 20th Street. Another right onto Ninth Avenue. Whether the tycoon is going to dinner or just going home he is, of course, going to Alphabet City. Apparently every person in New York below the age of thirty goes to the Alphabet City.

The car eventually stops on Saint Mark's and Avenue A. Abosch is home. Or possibly at a friend's home. Or possibly at a girlfriend's home. Or…it doesn't matter. Whatever might come next is what matters.

Shortly I'm tailing Simon's car on the East River Drive, heading north. A fairly heavy snow begins. I stay "glued by two." I learned that this is the expression for tailing a car while allowing one other car in front of you for camouflage.

Simon exits the Drive and starts moving west all the way across Manhattan, then north on the Henry Hudson Parkway, across the Henry Hudson Bridge into the Bronx.

My tour guide, Detective Katherine Burke, explains the Bronx to me in two easy sentences.

"Riverdale is the fancy-ass part of the Bronx. Everything else is meh."

Traffic lightens, then slows. The snow dusts the road. "Glued by two" has to end. Now I keep some space behind Simon. He pulls off the main road, crosses even farther east. The street sign says "Independence Avenue." Then Simon pulls into a long circular driveway of a very elegant apartment building.

Two men come out of the building. One is clearly a doorman—the hat, the coat, the gloves. The other is smaller, in a black wool pea coat, a dark woolen ski cap pulled down over his head.

Simon hands the doorman a very large, flat, wrapped package.

"You don't have to be a detective to figure out that Simon just gave the doorman a painting," says Burke. "I wonder if…"

But I interrupt her. I speak loudly.

"Son of a bitch!" I say.

"What's the matter?"

"The other man," I say.

We watch as Simon hands the other man a similar-looking wrapped package.

"Do you know him?" she asks.

"I sure as hell do."

"Who is he?" asks Burke.

"It's the little guy on the back elevator. It's Angel Corrido."

CHAPTER 16

ANGEL AND THE DOORMAN carry the paintings into the building. The doorman returns immediately. Angel remains inside.

We watch Simon and the doorman closely. They seem to be having a very intense conversation. The pantomime goes like this: The doorman moves close to Simon. The doorman looks like he is screaming. Then it appears that Simon is having none of it. Simon, using both hands, pushes the doorman. Although the doorman is larger than Simon, and the shove doesn't seem particularly violent, the doorman staggers backward and falls to the sidewalk.

As the doorman staggers to his feet, Simon puts his hand in his coat pocket. I am expecting a knife or a gun to be pulled out. Instead he hands the doorman something I don't recognize.

"Looks like Simon may have just slipped the doorman some cash," I say.

"I'm not sure, Moncrief. He handed him something. It looked like a tiny package."

"Some rolled-up bills," I say.

"No," says Burke. "My guess is he gave him a good noseful of coke." Then she adds, "And by the way, don't you think we should call him by his real name? He is *not* 'Preston Parker Simon.' He is Rudy Brunetti. Let's stop calling him Simon."

I think that this is a…what?…the kind of correction that Burke enjoys. Ah, well, it is easier for me to agree. So I nod. Then I say, "Brunetti it is."

Now we watch Simon…er, Brunetti…go back inside the building. The building doorman gets into the car and drives it into an attached building marked GARAGE.

He's back on the door in less than five. I immediately drive up to the building entrance.

"Who are you here to see, sir?" says the doorman, a very thin man, two days' growth, a dark stain on the lapel of his heavy brown coat.

He's only spoken a few words, but I can tell that he has an accent. My guess is Danish.

I lean across Burke and say, "We're here to see you."

"Me?" he says. And he looks genuinely confused. He blinks his eyes quickly. He wipes his lips with his gloved right hand.

"Yes, we'd like to talk to you about the gentlemen who you just assisted with the paintings.…" I begin.

"What paintings?" he says.

I realize that this guy has a bad attitude *and* a drug problem. I am sure that Burke is onto this also. The symptoms are simple and obvious—quivering hands, milky pink eyes, perspiration on his upper lip. Dirty, matted wisps of blond hair stick out from beneath his hat.

K. Burke gets out of the car and stands next to the doorman. She flashes her ID.

I get out of the car and stand next to Burke. I touch the inner suit pocket where I carry the Glock I'm not supposed to carry.

"NYPD, sir," she says. "We'd like to see some ID immediately."

"What for? For helping a tenant with packages?"

"No. Possible possession of drugs. ID, please," I say.

I don't know a bit of Danish, but I think this guy just taught me the Danish word for "Shit."

CHAPTER 17

THE DOORMAN-DRUGGIE'S NAME IS Peter Lund. He was in the Royal Danish Navy. He jumped ship seven years ago. I guess I can buy that story.

Early on in the interview he says, "Yes, I like the heroin too much." A minute later, with very little prodding from us, he adds, "And yes, it is possible that Mr. Brunetti and Mr. C. bring the works of art in and out of the apartment."

He rubs his lips.

Major rule of an interview: If a suspect starts talking, let him keep talking. Don't interrupt.

"Mr. Brunetti tips me generous, and he sometimes gives me my H, and it is none of my business to ask the tenant what are his parcels in and out. Not my job."

I believe him. Burke nods. A signal to me that she also believes him. Okay, now we know that Brunetti is storing artwork here. But we need more.

Then I have an idea, an idea that might get us information.

"It would be a great help if you would take us to see Mr. Brunetti's car," I say.

"But he would be angry," says Lund.

"Then you will be arrested for drug possession," says Burke. "How's that for a trade-off?"

"Come on," I say. "Show us where Brunetti's car is parked."

Lund answers quickly. "Which one?"

Three minutes later we are standing in the underground garage of 2737 Independence Avenue, Riverdale, Bronx, New York.

Peter Lund points to three identical black Escalades parked side-by-side-by-side. We look in the windows. Just the usual: black leather seats, high-tech dashboards. Burke takes a quick picture of the cars, the interiors, the plates. With one client, what does Brunetti need a fleet of SUVs for? This, and the involvement of Angel Corrido, suggests that the operation is bigger than we thought.

Burke tells Lund that we'll probably be back to talk some more. She suggests he try to stay as clean as he can *and* try to keep his mouth shut.

On the ride back to Manhattan, Burke says to me, "I'll do the write-up when we get back. We can't keep screwing around, avoiding Nick Elliott. We've got to build a file for him."

"Do you have reason to believe he's become impatient?" I ask.

"Yeah, I do. Let me read you a message." Then she reads from her cell phone: "What the hell are you two doing? Barney Wexler is up my ass. And the commissioner is standing right next to Wexler." Then Burke looks up at me and adds, "Maybe if you read your messages…"

"We will have something for him tomorrow. Next day at the latest," I say.

"No, Moncrief. We've got to get something to Elliott now."

"You are much too worried about the upper echelon, K. Burke."

"No. I'm worried that we are getting in way over our heads. Put a choke hold on your arrogance, Moncrief. We don't know for sure what we've got. Art forgeries? Drugs? It's time we got the rest of the team caught up."

"Give me one more day without any interference."

"No. Listen. It's not me. It's the case. We've got the facts—the stolen art, Rudy, Angel, a dead society dame, drugs. But we don't know where it's leading or how the hell to put it all together."

"I know how to put it together. Please, K. Burke. One more day to follow my arrogance. Please. Don't make me beg."

"You're not *begging* me, Moncrief. You're *bullshitting* me. But fine, I'll give you one more shot, one more day to piss in the ocean. Then we call in the cavalry."

CHAPTER 18

ETIENNE DUCHAMPS IS a billionaire and a very important art collector. He is also my friend. I have known Etienne since we were both four years old and attended *la petite école*.

Etienne has arranged a private viewing of the Monet at the Namanworth Gallery. Only the best of customers receive this kind of treatment.

I tell K. Burke that she and I will be introduced to the gallery owners as Mr. and Mrs. Luc Moncrief, *les amis intimes de Monsieur Duchamps*. Burke is angry with such a charade. She is even angrier by what I say next.

"So, it would be good for you to dress in the style of a wife of a man who can afford to purchase a Monet," I say.

"In that case I'll wear clean chinos," she says, then curls her lips with annoyance.

Amazingly, when she shows up at my apartment the next morning she looks…well…*chic*. In fact, *très chic*. Slim black slacks, black silk blouse, beige cashmere cardigan sweater. Her black hair is shiny, piled up fashionably carelessly. A brown silk scarf and a short sheared beaver jacket pull the look together.

"What have you done with Katherine Burke?" I say as I open the door.

"Don't expect me to ever look like this again, Moncrief. Everything but my underwear is borrowed from my friend Christine, who happens to be a buyer at Neiman Marcus."

"You look like a woman who has a château that is chock-full of Monets. But I would add one or two little touches, if Madame Moncrief does not mind."

"What exactly are those 'touches'?"

"You'll see in a moment." Then I walk into my bedroom and quickly return.

"Here, put these on," I say.

I hand her a bracelet with two rows of twenty small square-cut diamonds on each row. The clasp that keeps it together fastens onto a large citrine stone. I also hand her a thin gold chain from which hangs an antique ruby and diamond pendant.

"This type of jewelry is what my mother used to call 'daytime jewelry,'" I say, forcing a smile.

"I don't feel comfortable wearing these things," she says, as I help her with the necklace clasp.

"You look exactly like the wife of a wealthy art collector," I say. Then I look away from her.

"Moncrief," she says. "I can't. Didn't this jewelry belong to…?"

"Yes, of course. But they have been sitting like sad orphans in Dalia's jewelry safe," I say.

Is my voice cracking? Can Burke hear my heart beating? What the hell am I doing?

"Think about this. It's not right," Burke says.

I glance at her. She does look lovely. Then I speak loudly.

"Enough with the jibber-jabber. Let's go," I say. "We have a Monet to examine."

CHAPTER 19

THE OWNERS, SOPHIA and Andre Krane, are waiting for us at the shop door.

"I drove in from the country this morning. I so wanted to greet you myself," Sophia Krane says. She is a phony, but the kind that Dalia used to call "a *real* phony."

Sophia looks to be about seventy-five years old. Elegant, well-preserved, slow-moving, fake-golden hair pulled back tight. She says she's a countess. Even if she is lying, she carries herself like royalty.

Her husband, Andre, must be at least ten years older. Andre is not nearly so well-preserved. Overweight, balding, he wears a herringbone sports jacket with leather elbow patches. Later K. Burke will say, "The coveted New England college professor look."

The Monet has been moved from the window to a large easel. It is a wonder of the impressionist's art. When we stand close to the canvas we see a blur of overlapping colors, a clown's scarf, a paint-by-numbers set. A few steps back the viewer is transported to a breathtakingly beautiful field in Giverny.

Just as Sophia Krane appears to be a real countess, so too does this painting appear to be a real Monet. But what do I know?

Burke and I are not there as art experts; we are there as sniffing-around detectives.

Andre Krane speaks: "And how does Madame Moncrief like the piece?"

To my astonishment Burke speaks with a graceful and very believable French inflection. I am amazed at her acting. I've seen her "play" tough. I've seen her "play" sentimental, but I've never seen her transform herself into a woman of high society.

"As expected, it is magnificent," Burke says, a charming and slight smile enhancing her performance.

"I will tell you," says Sophia, "that we have had an offer of forty. The offer is from an American, seventy-five percent is in cash, the remainder in stock holdings…dot-com stock, of course."

"Of course," Burke says.

I nod and stifle the urge to stroke my chin in contemplation.

"Not to change the subject too much," I say, "but are you by chance representing any of the Moderns?"

"Not many," says Andre.

"A minor Utrillo," says Sophia. "A few other things."

Andre speaks conspiratorially, lowering his voice. "Follow us. We'll take you someplace very special—the Back Room. It's where we keep the work that we don't show just anybody."

CHAPTER 20

THE "BACK ROOM" turns out to be nothing more than a kind of storage space. On the near wall are two unframed canvases. Both have the graffiti touch of a Basquiat. Sophia Krane flicks her hand dismissively toward the unframed pieces.

"You won't want these," she says. "They're second-rate examples. I knew Basquiat well."

As if to prove her friendship, she now refers to him by his first name. "Jean-Michel has much better work. We just don't have any of it at the moment."

Then she walks to three framed canvases on the floor. They lean against the opposite wall, behind one another.

"Now these…" she says. Andre flips on an overhead fluorescent bulb. Sophia continues in her casual tone.

"This is a good Hopper. It comes from a private collection in Philadelphia. I think there was something going on between Hopper and the woman who originally owned it."

She slides the painting to the side. She reveals a three-dimensional painting of a toy fire truck.

"Feldman. He's hot again," says Sophia.

"Whoever thought he'd be back on top?" says her husband. Sophia shoots Andre a mean glance, then says, "I did, darling."

The third painting is a series of bowls on a shelf—simple, geometric, flat.

Sophia speaks.

"Ed Baynard is back, too. At least he's back for the wealthy couples in Sanibel and Palm Beach. The rich people in Florida can't decorate a media room without one of these pretty little Baynards hanging near their recliner chairs."

Sophia's art lesson has ended, and, although I find the Baynard paintings quite appealing, I am smart enough to remain silent.

Suddenly my fake–French wife speaks.

"I really would like to look at them further…but at a later time," Burke says. "Luc and I are meeting our mutual friend, Etienne, for drinks…."

"Etienne is in town? I didn't know that," says Andre.

Burke is, I think, becoming a bit too impressed by her own charade. We need to get out. Burke speaks.

"Just for the day. An unexpected business meeting. So we will be in touch about the Monet and perhaps the Feldman. But, you know, I do have a question."

"Of course," says Sophia.

Burke continues.

"Isn't it unusual to have such valuable pieces stacked one on top of another, leaning against the wall, on a dirty floor?"

"That's how the artists often keep them in their studios," says Andre.

"But this is not a studio," Burke says, her charming smile in place.

Detective Burke and Mrs. Krane exchange tense smiles. But I know Burke well enough to realize that she is heading somewhere in this conversation.

"I was so hoping," she says, "that you would sift through those three paintings and reveal a fourth canvas. I was foolishly hoping for a piece by Frida Kahlo. One of the self-portraits."

"Yes, everyone loves the self-portraits," says Andre. "The perfect scarves, the interesting headdress…"

"You know…" says Sophia.

"I know what you're thinking," says Andre. (I prepare myself for an avalanche of bullshit.)

Sophia speaks directly to K. Burke. Here it comes.

"You know, there is a collector, a very discreet individual, who has acquired three Kahlos over the years. The collector is away for the Christmas holidays. Saint Martin, I think. The French side, of course. I can get in touch, though. Would you be interested?"

"It would be a dream come true for Madame Moncrief," I say.

Burke touches my shoulder. She smiles at me. She speaks.

"What a sweet Christmas gift that could be…." Her voice trails off. And we say our good-byes.

As soon as we step onto 57th Street I say, "A magnificent performance, K. Burke."

"I'd like to thank the Academy…." she says. "And we might get a fake Frida Kahlo piece out of this."

But I am already plotting our next steps.

"I hope you are not too exhausted for tonight's job, when we follow Simon again," I say.

"No, we're not flying solo anymore. It's time to brief Elliott on our suspicions."

"Tonight will be our last time, K. Burke," I say.

"No way," says Burke. "No freakin' way." She is angry.

I smile my most charming smile and say, "Tonight if we get Simon we will be able to arrest him."

Burke speaks slowly, firmly.

"If you go on surveillance again, Moncrief, you're doing it without me."

I speak, barely able to spit out the words. I am angry also.

"If that's the way you want it, then stay back tonight. Stay and punch the numbers, search the file. I will do real police work. Go on back to Elliott now. Tell him whatever you like. As for me, I'm going into the Sherry-Netherland for a martini."

CHAPTER 21

I SIT WITH a frosty gin martini—straight up—at the bar of the Sherry-Netherland. The happy quiver of the first sip calms me, at least for a moment. Then my phone buzzes. A message from K. Burke. She texts: Read this. Then call me or come to precinct.

I read the following, from the *New York Post*'s website:

BYE-BYE, BABY D

Mrs. Ramona Driver Dunlop, the society matron known popularly as "Baby D," was bid farewell today at a lavish memorial service at St. Thomas Episcopal Church on Fifth Avenue and 53rd Street. White lilies and Bach cantatas filled the air as friends and family remembered the glamorous life of the social queen. Understandably, none of the speakers mentioned Baby D's earthly farewell—a particularly gruesome murder.

"There are more detectives and cops here than there are friends," said nightlife gossip blogger Teddy Galperin. "Let's hope one of them can finally make some headway in the case."

His comment was a reference to the NYPD's inability to make any progress in solving the murder of Mrs. Dunlop Friday. NYPD has thus far offered no clues as to the story behind the grisly death of the elderly woman.

In her youth Mrs. Dunlop was named New York Debutante of the Year. In recent years, the wealthy widow had turned her considerable energy and fortune to helping charities involved with the scourge of drug abuse. A lover and collector of fine art, Mrs. Dunlop also served on the boards of many museums, including the Frick and the Metropolitan Museum of Art. She is survived by her son and daughter-in-law.

I do not call K. Burke. I know what she will tell me: *No more screwing around, Moncrief! We must get help!*

I text K. Burke: Hold Elliott off until tomorrow. Don't be angry.

Burke texts me back: Not angry. Just worried.

CHAPTER 22

I'M WAITING EXACTLY where I waited the previous night. But this time, I'm waiting in the car that Dalia had christened "The Baby Blue from '62." And K. Burke isn't here to tell me that driving a flashy Corvette is a foolish idea.

Simon/Brunetti sits in his Escalade. The "rich kid" comes out of the building and slides into the backseat. When they take off, I take off after them.

Okay. A slight variation this time around: Simon deposits Abosch at Dirt Candy, a hip vegetarian restaurant on Allen Street.

This time Simon heads back to the Henry Hudson, only we take the George Washington Bridge into New Jersey. Simon speeds…85…90….I speed too. It seems like Simon knows all the speed traps. He slows down three times, always unexpectedly. Then back up to 85…90….The Baby Blue from '62 and I are loving it. *Detective Burke, you don't know what you're missing.*

An hour and a half later, we're in Monticello, New York. A few minutes later we're maneuvering around dark roads in the Catskills.

I turn off my headlights and drop back to a safe distance. The guardrails and ditches on the country roads become my guide. If I lose track of Simon's car, I'll be adrift.

Occasionally I see a house decorated with Christmas lights. A few Nativity scenes on front lawns. Neon wreaths. But mostly murky darkness.

Ten…fifteen…twenty minutes. Amazingly at a certain point I see Simon's car flash a right-turn signal. Is it a driver's reflex? Or, as Americans say: Is this guy just messing with me?

CHAPTER 23

A TOUCH OF winter moonlight provides just enough illumination to watch the Escalade pull into a very long dirt driveway. At the end of the driveway is a large Tudor-style mansion. I park on the road.

Two in the morning, but most of the windows are bright with lights. Simon leaves his car. He carries two packages. I'm assuming that they're the same paintings from last evening in Riverdale. But why drop them in storage instead of coming straight here? Maybe for discretion.

He rings the doorbell and looks around him. Yup, he's nervous. In a few moments Andre Krane opens the door. Simon disappears inside.

Now I exit my car. I stretch. I step into the woods a few feet. I survey the area. Woods and woods and then more woods. Giant trees—bare oaks, bare elms, hundreds of pines and evergreens. Tiny-sized to majestic-tremendous. The ground is covered with snow, tree limbs peeking out. Not far from the house is an ice-gray lake. More evergreens surround the lake, a lake so big that I can't even tell where it ends.

I return to the car and open the glove compartment. I unwrap a perfectly ripe piece of Camembert. I push a piece of sliced baguette into the soft cheese and enjoy my meal. A crisp Belgian ale, a perfect heirloom apple. A good snack along with this simple fact: I love solo detective work so much that even these bizarre and boring stakeouts are enjoyable to me. I'm a hunter after the game. There is a prize at the end for my perfect patience.

I crack the car window open an inch. The cold air rushes in.

Then I turn on the engine and warm the car. This on-and-off engine procedure occurs four times in the next hour. My eyes remain fixed on the house. I watch the lights go out. The mansion is draped in darkness. But I will not sleep.

At three o'clock I exit the car again. I bend and touch my toes a few times. I tie my silk scarf snug around my neck and chin. The snow begins again. The night is relentlessly cold.

I decide to move closer to the Krane house. *Histoire de voir.* I'll see what I can see.

CHAPTER 24

THROUGH THE LEAD-FRAMED windows of the dining room, when my eyes adjust to the dark, I see a giant oak table with chairs that look like Tudor thrones. If I expected to see a Matisse or an O'Keeffe hanging on the wall, I am disappointed. Four British fox-hunting prints. Nothing else.

I walk to the rear of the house and look into the huge kitchen. Two old stoves. Two deep sinks. A refrigerator from the 1950s. A marble-topped pastry table. A butler's pantry.

The ground is frozen hard, yet beneath the snow are deep hidden holes. I look toward the lake. The dock is covered with layers of tarp.

I move cautiously through the ice and snow. I now stand at the windows to the living room. Nothing on the wall except some African carvings and bronze antique sabers.

I decide to head back to my car. Too cold. Too icy. Also I must be there if Simon suddenly leaves.

I hear the door to the house open, and voices. There he is. I begin to run—then I trip. A hole? A branch? A discarded fake Picasso? I am not hurt. I get up quickly. But my fall has apparently tipped someone off to my presence.

Suddenly the unmistakable sound of a bullet cracks the air. It shatters a piece of the stucco wall near where I stand and lands significantly away from where I'm standing. But a bullet can never land far enough away.

Then another bullet.

Another shot. Because the woods appear thicker near the lake I try to run there as fast as possible. To hide. To escape. I take out my gun, but I'm not acting in a Western. Real life offers no chance for me to spin on my heels and actually shoot my pursuer.

My knees are bent. I run close to the ground. If I fall I have less chance of getting hurt.

Then a scream in the darkness.

"I *will* get you, Moncrief."

The dumbest detective in America could identify the British-sounding voice. It is, of course, Preston Parker Simon/Rudy Brunetti.

I keep running as fast as possible toward the lake. What once looked like a short distance seems like a marathon challenge.

Another bullet. Then immediately another.

My shoes and ankles and calves are soaked with melted snow and ice.

Another bullet.

As I get closer to the lake, a voice comes at me: "You'd better be able to swim that lake, asshole." He's stalling. Probably reloading.

Simon is closer. But now he sounds simpler, cruder, American. I get it. He's slipped into being his real self. He's not Preston Parker

Simon. He's Rudy Brunetti. Now I am at the water's edge. In the dim moonlight I can see Simon. He is getting closer.

He fires three more bullets in succession. The bullets land close enough to where I stand that I can see sections of the icy surface shatter.

He fires two more shots.

He suddenly shouts, "Who the hell…? Angel, is that you?"

No response.

"Angel? Angel?"

Still no response.

Another yell from Simon: "Krane. Is it you? Are you there?"

I can see Simon clearly now. I watch him raise his gun. He fires in my direction. He fires again. He misses. He aims carefully. I fall to the snowy icy ground. He lowers his aim just a bit. He sees me.

He raises his arm slightly. He reevaluates the situation.

I am like a scared child. I close my eyes tightly.

Then…one more bullet shot. It comes nowhere near me.

I wait for the next bullet. And I wait. I only hear the sounds of nature. Winter birds cackling in the sky. Strong winds whipping through the pine trees.

Then a voice calls out.

"You okay, Moncrief?"

I know that voice. It is K. Burke.

CHAPTER 25

THE CHEESY TUDOR-STYLE living room—like something out of Disneyland—fills up quickly with lots of local law enforcement.

The New York State police arrive: seven burly men and two substantial-looking women. The local Monticello police arrive: two detectives, two coroners, four police officers. This may be the entire town police department. The local press arrives, as eager and noisy as anything in Manhattan or Paris. The coroners do a quick on-site examination of Rudy Brunetti. Then they begin to transfer the body to an ambulance.

I stand at an open window and watch them speedily move the body to the ambulance. The coroner sees me and explains what I already know: "We need to minimize dermal contamination."

Why do American officials enjoy using big words? Couldn't he just have said "skin decay"?

Detective Burke and I are at different corners of the room. We see each other, and I immediately join my colleague, the person who just saved my life.

"So, K. Burke," I say. "You *did* accompany me after all." I squeeze her shoulders, as close to a loving gesture as we have ever shared.

"You probably predicted that I'd be following you," she says.

I tell her the truth.

"Not this time, I must say. This time I thought our disagreement was too great for it to mend quickly."

There is a pause. Then she looks at me with intense eyes. Softly she says, "I could never let you down, Moncrief."

My head turns to the ground. My throat aches with anxiety. I know that I should be lying dead on the icy ground. I shake. My neck hurts. I speak.

"*Merci, merci beaucoup.* You have saved my life. I am beyond grateful."

Burke smiles. Her eyes sparkle.

"As you should be."

I smile. This will not grow any further into a sentimental moment. That is simply not the way Burke and I behave.

And anyway, we must not allow the local police to take over. No. Now we must take control, as all the little puzzle pieces of the investigation begin to fall into place.

The results turn out to be fairly much as we expected. The elegant Sophia and Andre Krane are the masterminds in this grand fraud scheme. They maintain a large basement studio at this home. It looks like a classroom at a university's fine arts painting course. Easels with half-finished canvases dot the room—a large Picasso here, a tiny Rubens there, a Schnabel that looks like every other Schnabel, a Warhol "Liz Taylor" that looks like a thousand others.

Handcuffs are locked onto the Kranes. Sophia Krane is calm,

stoic, almost bored, as she stands with three police officers guarding her.

"Rudy was a fool. I told him all he had to do was steal some goddamn paintings, from her bedroom. He didn't have to kill the old lady," she says.

"But he did," K. Burke says.

Now the Kranes are led out of their gloomy house to join Angel, who is already in a police car.

Burke and I question and Andre quickly admits that they sold the Hockney and Lichtenstein forgeries to Baby D. Only too eager to sell out their pal Rudy, he described how they had planted him—already an accomplice in art forgery sales—as her driver, when other clients of the gallery had started to raise alarm about the legitimacy of their pieces.

Rudy was supposed to gain access and steal the paintings back, but she'd sniffed him out and fired him before he had the opportunity. Desperate, after their last drive Rudy had killed her—but was too cowardly to take the paintings then, sniffed Sophia.

So they'd enlisted Angel Corrido to "retrieve" them from the apartment after her death. Their fear at that point, of course, had become that Mrs. Dunlop's estate would identify the pieces as forgeries. "You might as well look in Baby D's second maid's room," Sophia tells us. "She has a box spring with a secret compartment. Right now you'll probably find a Giotto wood panel and a group of architectural drawings from Horace Walpole's country home that Angel couldn't manage to get out. And…oh, yes…ten animation cels from Disney's *Snow White and the Seven Dwarfs*."

"No one can say we don't offer a variety," says Andre.

The local chief of police, the Monticello district attorney, and the sergeant of the county police approach us like a pumped-up sports team. I know what they want: a quarrel. Will these three criminals be tried in Sullivan County where they were arrested? Or will they be tried in Manhattan where their crimes were committed? I'm way too weary to deal with this.

"K. Burke, you have given me the greatest gift that one person can possibly give another. Thanks to you, I am still alive."

"All in a day's work," she says, with only a trace of irony in her voice.

"Now I must ask for one more favor, a small favor," I say.

She simply rolls her eyes.

"What is it, Moncrief? Do you want me to give you a kidney?"

"Actually, worse than that. Would you please deal with these three local police people? I have an errand to run."

"An errand? It's five thirty in the morning. We're at a crime scene in the middle of the woods a hundred miles from home base...and you've got an errand to run?"

"*Merci,* K. Burke. *Merci, merci,* and for good luck, one more *merci.*"

CHAPTER 26

IT IS DARK as midnight when I walk outside. The late-November morning is misty and cold. It is snowing lightly, just enough to make the air wet and icy. It is a perfect environment for sadness. The frozen lake, the dark night, the icy air…it should be ideal for depression. Yet I am strangely buoyant. I am calmer than I have been in months. I know it is the result of a successful end to the art forgery case. The usual sense of smugness that runs through me is stronger than ever. I look forward to discussing the details with Elliott. I know that some of my New York colleagues will have a touch of envy that this French interloper cracked the case. But most of all I am deeply warmed by Katherine Burke's extraordinary role in saving my life. Beyond friendship, and even, in a certain way, beyond romantic love.

I look down toward the lake. I stand still. I imagine the scene of a few hours ago, a scene of terror as a man with a gun pursued me through the dark. Now the entire area is one of peace and beauty.

A wooden shed sits not far from the main house. I have seen sheds like this outside some of the very old châteaux of France; they are remnants from hundreds of years earlier—outdoor bathrooms, basically toilets for the servants.

I look through the one small glass window in the shed's wooden door. The tiny household's gardening equipment—old-fashioned hand mowers, clippers, axes, shovels. I open the door and see a rusty bow saw hanging on a hook. I take it down and walk toward the lake.

In this forest of dead winter branches and hundreds of evergreens, I find a pine tree that is precisely the same height as myself—six feet, no taller, no shorter. It is not a tree from a storybook—not a scrawny lonely tree, yet not a great thick beauty. A tree. Simple. Lovely. A good representation of the work of God…if you are happy enough with life to still believe in God.

The trunk is soft. I cut through easily. As I do, I notice how completely ruined my shoes and trousers are—stained with water and ice and snow and the feces of deer and dogs.

I give the severed trunk an easy shove, and the tree falls forward. Just as I slip the bow saw over my shoulder and lift the bottom end of the trunk to drag the tree back toward the house, I hear a man's voice calling.

He shouts my name. He calls, "Detective Moncrief. Over here."

I wave at him, and he continues toward me. I recognize him as one of the Monticello police officers on the crime scene. He is no boy. He may be as old as thirty. As he comes closer I see that he is tall and blond and handsome, no doubt a local girl's dream.

But as is always the way with me, I am hesitant, suspicious. Perhaps the Kranes and Rudy Brunetti had a cabal of helpers up here. It would not be incredible—a few facilitators in the police force, in city hall, in the highway department.

I drop the tree and slip the bow saw from my shoulder to my hand. I grip the saw handle tightly.

The police officer stands next to me.

"I can give you a hand with that," he says. "I saw you from way up there."

"Ah, you caught me in the act of thievery," I say.

"I think you can help yourself to anything you want around here. You and Detective Burke are heroes. This is pretty amazing, the way you solved this case."

He nods his head nervously. He looks a bit goofy.

"Persistence," I say. "All it takes is persistence…and a great deal of patience."

"Yeah, I'm sure," he says. Then he speaks quickly.

"I was talking to your partner," he says. "Um…I asked her… well, I hope you won't be mad, but I asked her if you and her were anything more than partners."

I know exactly what the young man means, but I pretend otherwise.

"More than partners?" I ask.

"You know…God, I can't believe I'm doing this…like…" He cannot get it out.

"What did Detective Burke say?" I ask.

"She said 'absolutely not,' but then she told me to ask you."

"She is teasing you, *monsieur*. Detective Burke and I are partners professionally, but we are just friends."

"Just friends," he repeats. "So I could see her, go on a date with her?"

"You could go to the moon with her," I say.

"I'll help you with the tree," he says. Then he adds, "You take the lighter end."

"I'm fine with this end," I say. So we carry the tree. I see K. Burke is standing, waiting for us near the toolshed.

"*That's* where you were, Moncrief. Cutting down a tree?" she says with a smile. "I can't believe it."

The police officer, K. Burke, and I are standing, admiring the tree.

"Christmas is a few weeks away, K. Burke. Here is my gift to you. For Christmas and for saving my crazy little life. We can tie the tree to the roof of the car and bring it back to the city. This strapping young man can help us."

She looks at me. I speak.

"Merry Christmas, Detective," I say.

"Merry Christmas, Detective," she says.

Then K. Burke begins to cry. I also feel my eyes fill with tears.

The young police officer speaks.

"Just friends," he says. "Sure. Just friends."

CHAPTER 27

CHRISTMAS IS COMING. And as my favorite American expression goes: I couldn't care less.

In the past I would have been in deep consultation with Miranda, my traditional Cartier shopping assistant. Miranda had a 1.000 batting average in helping me select the perfect Christmas gift for Dalia. Not too flashy, but not too boring. Something with sparkle, but something that did not call attention to itself…like Dalia herself.

It is December 20, and whatever gift-giving I am doing these few days is taken care of with a checkbook. I write gift checks for the daily maid, the twice-a-week laundress, the wine merchant at Astor who advises me when a particular Bordeaux is at its peak, Xavier who cuts my hair at Roman K, and…and that is it.

I consider giving something special to Detective Burke. But what do you give a person who has saved your life? An expensive car, an expensive trip, an expensive bracelet? They each sound ridiculous, and I think perhaps that any of them would insult Katherine Burke.

The days since the arrests of the art forgery gang have been dull. Elliott suggested that we take some time off. I tried to do so, but a man can only play so much squash and attend so many exhibitions at MoMA and the Morgan.

K. Burke takes a few days to do some Christmas shopping with her nieces and nephews in New Jersey. I decline to accompany them to the Short Hills Mall.

When we return to work we catch up on the paperwork for the forgery case. We make an easy arrest of a drug dealer outside Julia Richman High School on East 67th Street. Elliott asks us to spend two days renewing our former Bloomingdale's assignment. We are reluctant and grumpy and unpleasant about the assignment, but the department store is a block away from Le Veau d'Or, where we have lunch this afternoon. The impeccably old-fashioned French restaurant on 60th Street still knows how to make perfect veal kidneys in a mustard sauce. And this afternoon Le Veau d'Or becomes the first (and most likely, last) restaurant where K. Burke has her first taste of *tripes à la mode de Caen*. When I tell her that tripe is the stomach lining of a cow, she simply shrugs and says, "All I know is that it tastes good. Thanks for the reco." I think she is lying. But such a lie means that she must finish eating the dish.

Bloomingdale's closes at 10:00 p.m. Fifteen minutes later I am sitting in my apartment, sifting through Christmas cards wishing me *Joyeux Noël et Bonne Année*.

I stand and pour myself a small glass of Pepto-Bismol. Have I grown too old for veal kidneys?

The phone rings. The Caller ID shows the familiar 161 area code for Paris, but the remainder of the phone number means nothing to me.

As I reach for the phone I remember that it is about five in the morning in Paris.

"Luc," she says. "It is Babette."

Babette Moreau is my father's personal secretary. She has been his secretary for forty years, maybe longer.

My instincts tell me why she is calling.

"Votre père est mort."

Your father has died.

My first instinct is to feign sadness. I do not want Mademoiselle Babette to have proof of what she already knows: my father and I had a distant, sometimes angry relationship. He was a man of great financial achievement and great emotional distance. Early on—when it became clear that he and I had nothing in common except that we were related—he, a young widower, dispatched me to the care of nannies and tutors and tennis instructors and private schools. He thought that my interest in police work was ridiculous, and, while he was extremely generous with his money, he was extremely sparing with his love and companionship. This system worked. He did not care much about me. And I surely did not care very much about him.

A different son might burst into tears. A different son might express over-the-top shock at the news. But I am not that son. And I am a detective, not an actor.

"A heart attack," Babette says. "No pain. He was at his desk, of course."

"Of course," I say.

"The arrangements?" I ask.

"Notre Dame," she says. "That is what he would have wanted."

"Yes," I reply. "That is certainly what he would have wanted."

A pause, and then she asks what she is afraid to ask.

"Will you attend?" she says.

I do not pause.

"Of course," I say. It is an honest response. No, I am not moved by his death. But for a son not to attend his father's funeral is an extraordinary offense.

I tell her that I will leave tomorrow for Paris. She tells me that she will schedule the funeral after my arrival. I tell her to call me if there is anything else I need to know. The conversation ends.

What do I do next? I telephone K. Burke.

"That's awful, Moncrief," she says. Then a pause. Then… "Listen. I know you and your father didn't have the best relationship. But *he was your father*. Nothing changes that. Do you want me to come by and be with you?"

"No," I say. "No. But there is something you can do to help me through this."

"Of course. What is it?"

"Tomorrow afternoon…come to Paris with me."

CHAPTER 28

"I AM EMBARRASSED to be enjoying this flight so much," says K. Burke.

The premier cabin is spacious and elegant. Aside from an exotic-looking sheik who is traveling with a valet, Burke and I are the only other passengers in the first-class compartment of this Air France flight to Paris. The luxury is, even for a spoiled brat like me who has flown first class his entire life, extraordinary. It is slightly intoxicating to be above the Atlantic Ocean with so much *stuff* at one's disposal: flatbed seats for perfect sleeping, each bed with a small dressing room attached; perfectly chilled bottles of Dom Pérignon; access to first-run movies.

"And you are embarrassed…why?" I ask.

"Because we are going to Paris for a funeral. Not a wedding, not a birthday party, not even a business meeting. A funeral."

"Just pretend that it is one of the pleasanter events you just mentioned," I say. "Or call it business. I'm certain business will be discussed. I have already received two emails from my late father's personal assistant Babette and *three* emails from his protégé, Julien Carpentier."

"Julien Carpentier," Burke repeats. "That's a new name for me."

"Julien is his 'business assistant.' Julien is the new and improved version of the son I was supposed to be. If I had turned out to be the person my father wished me to be—ambitious, serious, businesslike—I would have been Julien. Instead I became what my father called *un policier fou*, a foolish policeman."

"And Julien is an asshole, I suppose?" K. Burke asks as she piles a generous spoonful of beluga caviar onto a warm blini.

"Surprisingly not. I do not know him well, but the few times I've seen or spoken with Julien, he has been quite…I don't know the word precisely…pleasant…authentic…yes, that is it, authentic. I think he is happy with his luck to have such an important position. Plus he diverts my father's attention from me. Julien and Babette are both probably truly saddened by my father's death. While you and I are sitting in luxury, sipping the bubble-water, soon to go to sleep on Pratesi bed linens, Julien is tending to the comings and goings of the company."

The flight attendant stops at our seats. She is carrying the 500mg tin of beluga with her. Pointing at the tin with her mother-of-pearl caviar spoon, she asks if we would like some more.

Burke hesitates.

"Go ahead," I say. "Have some more. Caviar builds strength. You will need all you can get for our important meetings."

I smile, but the flight attendant takes my remarks seriously.

"Ah, you are in France on business?" she says.

"In a manner of speaking," I say.

"I hope you will meet with great success," she says.

When the pretty young woman leaves us, Detective Burke speaks.

"By the way, Moncrief. I did do something that *you* forgot to do," she says.

"Whatever we failed to pack will be available at my father's house," I say.

"Don't be so smug. It's nothing as simple as dental floss or underwear. You forgot to tell Inspector Elliott that we are disappearing for three days."

"We are not *disappearing,* K. Burke. We are on holiday," I say.

"Well, maybe you can be cavalier about this. But not me. I need this job. Anyway, I called Elliott earlier and told him that he was right, we both needed a real break, that the work from the forgery case finally caught up with us. So we were taking a few days off."

"And he said what?"

"He said 'You two guys deserve it. Have fun.'"

I begin to laugh. Burke looks confused. My laughter grows louder.

"What's so funny, Moncrief?"

"Don't you see? Our boss thinks that we're off on a romantic journey."

I keep on laughing. Detective Burke does not.

CHAPTER 29

EIGHT O'CLOCK IN the morning at Charles de Gaulle airport.

Burke and I are fast-tracked through customs. We are suffering from "Dom Pérignon Syndrome," an alcohol-fueled sleep followed by a walloping morning headache.

In the reception lounge K. Burke says to me, "There he is. There's Julien Carpentier." She points to a handsome man in his late twenties, perhaps his early thirties. Six feet tall or so. Light-brown hair. A well-cut, dark-blue overcoat, a dark-blue silk scarf.

"How did you know that man is Julien?" I ask. "You've never seen him before."

"Correct. But I know it's Julien Carpentier because he looks exactly like you."

It has been at least a year since I have seen Julien, but for some reason this time, in the bright unflattering light of the airport, I see the truth of K. Burke's observation. He is not a mirror image of me, not a twin, but we both have a sharp nose, straight long hair, green eyes.

Julien is accompanied by a beautiful woman who is formally dressed in a chauffeur's uniform—black suit, brass buttons, large

cap. I cannot help but think that this is the beginning of a porno-
graphic film.

Julien moves toward me quickly and embraces me like a
brother, which perhaps he thinks he is. I return the hug with a lot
less vigor.

"*Mon ami, Luc.* Welcome. Welcome." He turns to Katherine
Burke and makes a small quick bow from the waist. "And this, of
course, is Mademoiselle Burke, a fine companion to have at this
sorrowful time."

Julien takes Burke's hand, bows once again, and—well, he
doesn't quite *kiss* her hand—he gently *brushes* Burke's hand beneath his lips.

"I only wish that we might have met under happier circumstances," Julien says. K. Burke says that she agrees.

"Huguette and I will go gather your luggage," Julien says. "We
will meet you at the doorway marked D-E." As they leave for the
luggage carousel Burke mumbles, "No. Don't…it's all right. I…"
In the noise of the terminal they do not hear her.

"Let them go," I say. "We will have to listen to Julien chatter all
the ride into Paris. Let's take a short break from him right now."

"But, Moncrief. There's only one little suitcase, mine. You said
you didn't need to bring anything, that you had a lot of clothing
at your father's. Julien and that hot-looking driver are going to be
looking for your stuff. And then they'll…"

"Listen. I have only been with Julien about sixty seconds, and
he is already annoying me with yak-yak-yak."

"You're wrong. I think he's genuinely glad to see you. *And*

I think he's far more broken up about your father's death than you are."

"The woman who served us dinner on the plane was more broken up about my father's death than I am," I say.

I take a deep breath. I squeeze a few eyedrops into my eyes and say to K. Burke, "Very well. Let's go to the luggage area and find them. We'll tell them that we were so jet-lagged that we forgot we only had one small piece of luggage."

"You're impossible, Moncrief."

"Let's go find them, but…"

"But what?" Burke says.

"But let us walk very, very slowly."

CHAPTER 30

AS PREDICTED, JULIEN talks incessantly on the ride into Paris.

"Your father was a tough boss, but a fair boss."

"The factory workers in Lille and Beijing are all anxious about their future."

"*Monsieur le docteur* said the heart attack came fast. He did not suffer."

"I wanted the funeral at Sacré-Cœur. Babette wanted Notre Dame. She, of course, got her way. It is only right. She knew him best."

"The American ambassador, the ambassadors from Brazil and Poland, even the Russian ambassador, the one your father detested, will be there."

"We are prepared with security for the paparazzi. They will come for the television and cinema personalities."

"The presidents of *all* your father's offices are attending, of course."

"I am so grateful that the heart attack came quickly. Not that it was not expected after the two bypass surgeries and the ongoing atrial fibrillation."

"There will be a children's choir at the mass as well as the regular Notre Dame chorus."

K. Burke listens intently. I think she may actually be intrigued by the details of this grand affair. Julien and Babette have planned my father's funeral as if it were a royal wedding—red floral arrangements, Paris Archbishop André Vingt-Trois to officiate, Fauchon to cater the luncheon after the burial.

I tune out of Julien's lecture early on. His words come as a sort of sweet background music in my odd world of jet-lagged half sleep.

Then I hear a woman's voice.

"Luc," she says. "Luc," she repeats. It sounds very much like Burke's voice, but…well, she never uses my Christian name—"Luc." I am always "Moncrief" to her. She is always "K. Burke" to me.

"Luc," again. Yes, it *is* Burke speaking. I open my eyes. I turn my head toward her. I understand. With Julien and the driver here she will be using my first name. I smile and say, "Yes. What is it…Katherine?"

"Monsieur Carpentier asked you a question."

"I'm sorry. I must have dozed off," I say.

"Understandable. The jet lag. The long flight. The sadness," says Julien. "I merely wanted to know if you cared to stop and refresh yourselves at your father's house before we go to the *pompes funèbres* to view your father's body."

I have already told Burke that we would be staying at my father's huge house on rue de Montaigne, rather than my own apartment in the Marais. Burke knows the reason: I cannot go back to my own place, the apartment where I spent so many joyful days and nights with Dalia.

"Yes, I *do* want to go to the house," I say. "A bath, a change of clothes, an icy bottle of Perrier. Is that all right with you, *Katherine?*"

K. Burke realizes that I am having entirely too much fun saying her name.

"That's just perfect for me, *Luc.*"

"So, Julien," I say. "That's the plan. Perhaps we can allot a few hours for that, but then…well, I think we can hold off on the viewing of the body.…"

I pause and suppress the urge to add, *"My father will not be going anywhere."*

"I see," says Julien. "I just thought that you would…"

I speak now matter-of-factly, not arrogantly, not unpleasantly.

"Would this perhaps be a better expenditure of time instead to meet with Valex attorneys, get a bit of a head start on the legal work?" I ask.

"You're in charge, Luc," says Julien, but his voice does not ring with sincerity.

"Thank you," I say. "What I'd like you to do is assemble my father's legal staff. Invite Babette, of course. We can meet in my father's private library on the third floor. I am sure there are many matters they have to discuss with me. Ask anyone else who should be there to please be there. Only necessary people—division presidents, department heads. This may also be a convenient time to reveal the main points of the will."

Julien is furiously tapping these instructions into his iPad. I have one final thought.

"The important personages who are not here for the funeral—North America, A-Pac, Africa—Skype them in."

I am finished talking, but then K. Burke speaks up.

"What about other family members, Luc?" she asks.

There is a pause. Then Julien speaks.

"Luc is the only living family member."

"As I may have mentioned, *Katherine,* my father had two daughters and a son out of wedlock. I never met them. The girls are younger than I. The boy is a bit older. But arrangements have been made. Correct, Julien?"

"Correct. The lawyers settled trust funds upon them years ago," he says. He nods, but there is no complicit smile attached to the statement. "They have been dealt with quite a while ago."

Meanwhile Julien continues to tap away at his iPad. The car is now closing in on Central Paris. Julien looks up and speaks again.

"I have texted the IT staff. They are on their way to the house now. They will set up Skype and two video cameras, a backup generator…the whole thing."

"What about sleeping arrangements?" I ask. I look to see if there is a change of expression on Julien's face. Nothing.

"All the bedrooms are made up. You may, of course, do what you wish," says Julien.

"What I wish is for Mademoiselle Burke to have my old bedroom. It is quite large. It has a pleasant sitting room, and it looks out over the Avenue."

I look at Burke and add, "You will like it."

"I'm sure," she says.

"As for me, I will sleep in the *salon d'été*." The summer room. It is spacious and well-ventilated and close to my father's library. It was where I always slept during the summer months when I was a child. It is no longer summer. And I am no longer a child. But I can forget both those facts.

"Very well, Luc. As you wish. I will have a Call button installed, so you can summon a maid if you need one," Julien says as he flicks his iPad back on.

"Thank you," I say. "But that won't be necessary. I doubt if I'll have any need to summon a maid."

Julien smiles and speaks.

"As you wish, my friend."

CHAPTER 31

BABETTE ENTERS THE LIBRARY. She is dressed entirely in black, the whole mourning costume—stockings, gloves, even *une petit chapeau avec un voile.* Drama and fashion are her two passions, so my father's funeral is a glorious opportunity to indulge those interests.

"Luc. Mon petit Luc," she says loudly. She embraces me. She flips the short black veil from her forehead. Then she kisses me on both my cheeks. She is not an exaggerated comic character. She is, however, one of those French women trained to behave a certain way—formal, slightly over-the-top, unashamed.

She keeps talking.

"Mon triste petit bébé."

"I will agree to be your *bébé,* Babette, but not your '*sad* little baby.'"

She ignores what I say and moves on to a subject that will interest her.

"And this, of course, must be the very important police partner, Mademoiselle Katherine Burke of New York City."

"I'm delighted to meet you, Mademoiselle Babette," says K. Burke.

Detective Burke extends her hand to shake, but Babette has a different idea. She goes in for the double-cheek kiss.

The attorneys are arranging stacks of papers on the long marble table in the center of the room. Two of the housemaids, along with my father's butler, Carl, are arranging chairs facing that table. Three rows of authentic Louis XV chairs. We will be like an audience at a chamber music recital.

The attorneys introduce themselves to me. They extend their sympathies on "the loss of this magnificent man, your father." "He was one of the greats, the last of his kind."

One of the attorneys, Patrice LaFleur, the oldest person in the room, the only attorney I actually know, asks me if I would like to join him and his colleagues at the library table. I decline.

The doors to the book-lined room remain open. Well-dressed men and women enter and take seats.

"They are employees of Valex, important employees," Julien says.

Some of them smile at me. Some give a tiny bow.

"I'm a New York City cop, Julien. I'm not accustomed to such respect."

Julien Carpentier takes me by the shoulders. He looks directly into my eyes. He moves his head uncomfortably closer to mine. He speaks.

"This is a gigantic company. Sixteen offices. Twelve factories. Valex manufactures everything from antacids to cancer drugs. Thousands of people are dependent on Valex for their employment, hundreds of thousands are dependent on Valex for their health. You are their boss's son. *Allow* them to respect you."

I am a little nervous. I am a little confused.

"But this is not my company," I say. "It's my father's enterprise."

"But it is your responsibility," Julien says. I want very much to trust his sincerity, to trust Babette. But I have spent so much time in my life listening to the lies of heroin dealers and murderers that I cannot wholly embrace the sincerity of my father's two most trusted employees.

I nod at Julien. He smiles. Then I sit. Front row center. The best seat in the house.

Julien is to my left. K. Burke is to my right.

"What are you thinking, Moncrief?" whispers Burke.

"You know me too well, K. Burke. You can perceive that my instincts are telling me something."

The room is settling down. All is quiet. Burke leans in toward me. She whispers.

"Can you ask the lawyers to hold off for a few minutes, so you and I can talk?"

"No. What you and I have to say can wait."

CHAPTER 32

THE LEAD TRUSTS, wills, and estates attorney is Claude Dupain, a short-nosed, large-eared methodical little man who has devoted his entire life to my father's personal legal matters.

"Good afternoon to the family, friends, and business colleagues of my late great friend, Luc Paul Moncrief. Monsieur Moncrief's funeral memorial, as you know, will take place tomorrow. Today, however, at the request of his family, we are deposing of Luc's…forgive me…Monsieur Moncrief's will…forgive me once again…I am, of course, referring to Luc Moncrief père, Moncrief the elder. He is the Moncrief I shall be speaking of here.

"In the upcoming months, Monsieur Moncrief's bureau of attorneys will begin the complex filing of all business documents, debt documents, mortgages, and other Valex-related items. As you all know, Monsieur Moncrief paid strict attention to detail. While his death was terribly unexpected, he recently had become…shall we say…somewhat preoccupied with preparations for death. He brought his will and estate planning up to date in the last few weeks. And that recent planning is reflected in what I announce at this gathering.

"I must add that while it will take many months, even years, to honor all legal procedures in company matters, Monsieur Moncrief's wishes in other matters, personal matters and bequests, are quite simple and very clear."

I realize easily what Dupain's legal babble means: Valex is a monstrosity of a company, so it will take a great deal of time to sort out its future. However, my father's personal directions about his estate will be, like my father himself, easy to understand.

Dupain opens a leather portfolio and removes a few pieces of paper. I bow my head. I look down at the floor. The attorney speaks. And, as promised, the information is simple.

Babette will receive a yearly income of 150,000 euros with annual appropriate cost-of-living increases. She will also receive rent-free housing in her current house at Avenue George V. After her death, her heirs will receive the same annual amount for one hundred years.

Julien Carpentier is to continue at his annual salary of 850,000 euros annually. And, subject to the approval of the board of directors, Julien will be named Chairman and CEO of Valex and its subsidiaries.

The American phrase comes to mind again: I could not care less.

There now follows a long list—at least forty names—of disbursements to office personnel and household staff members in Paris, as well as at my father's London house, his château in Normandy, his house in Portofino, and—a stunning surprise to me—his apartment at 850 Fifth Avenue in New York.

The amounts of the disbursements are generous, excessive by

traditional standards. Housemaids will be able to stop scrubbing and dusting. Butlers will retire to Cannes. Gardeners will become country squires. Frankly, I am delighted for all of them.

After the listing of the bequeathals to the staff members, Dupain dabs at his forehead with a handkerchief. An assistant presents him with a large glass of ice water. He drinks the water in one long gulp. Then he says, "There is but one item left. I shall read it directly from Monsieur Moncrief's testament."

Dupain removes a single paper from yet another leather envelope. He reads:

"To my son, Luc Paul Moncrief, I leave all my homes and household goods, all attachments to those homes and household goods, all real estate, all attachments to that real estate. I further leave to him all monies and investments that I may own or control.

"*With the following stipulation:* After assigning this distribution to my son Luc Paul Moncrief, any monies remaining *in excess of three billion euros* will be divided equally among the Luc and Georgette Moncrief Foundation, the Louvre Museum, the Red Cross of France, and the Museum of Jewish Heritage in the United States."

There is a long pause, a very long pause. It is the kind of pause that comes when you hear that someone has just inherited three billion euros.

My head remains bowed. I continue to stare at the floor. The silence is punctuated by an occasional sob, a smattering of whispering. Finally, Dupain the attorney speaks again.

"I believe that it is now appropriate for the remainder of this meeting to be conducted, not by me, but by Luc Moncrief the younger."

I hold up my head. But I do not rise from my seat.

"Monsieur Dupain. I think that there is nothing more for me to add to the proceedings. However, I would like to ask a question of you," I say. "And I ask it here in the presence of all assembled, because it has troubled me since I was first informed of my father's death."

"But of course, monsieur."

"Are there police reports *or* medical reports *or* coroner reports *or* any kind of reports available concerning the death of my father?"

Dupain appears startled by the question, but he does not hesitate to answer.

"As you must know, Luc…er…Monsieur Moncrief, your father was a man in his late seventies. He had suffered from heart disease. He was discovered dead at his desk. Of course, there is an official death certificate signed by Doctor Martin Abel of the French Police Department."

"And that is all?" I ask.

"That is all that seemed necessary."

It is then…finally…that I feel my eyes fill with tears.

CHAPTER 33

WHEN I WAS YOUNGER, much younger—ten years old, fifteen years old—I visited magnificent homes of my school friends: huge châteaux in western France, thirty-room hunting lodges in Scotland, outlandishly large London town homes smack in the middle of Belgravia.

Many of these houses had rooms dedicated solely to pastimes like billiards and swimming and cigar-smoking and wine-tasting. Many had entire floors that housed ten to twenty servants. Some of the houses had stables with rooms put aside for tanning saddles and polishing stirrups.

But I had never seen in any other home the sort of room that we had in our house on rue du Montaigne.

Our house had a "silver room."

This room was about the size of a normal family dining room. It had perhaps fifty open shelves. These shelves were loaded with sterling silver serving pieces—everything from fingerbowls to soup tureens, asparagus servers to butter pats, charger plates the size of platters, water goblets as ornate as altar chalices. Open bins were neatly filled with stacks of dinnerware assorted into categories like "Cristofle" and "Buccellati" and "Tiffany." Subcategories were sets of silver dinnerware wrapped with red velvet ribbon, each bin marked with a note signifying when the pieces had been used:

1788, one year before the Revolution
1872, one year after the ending of the Franco-Prussian War
1943, a dinner for General Eisenhower and his secretary,
Kay Summersby
Babette, Birthday
Luc, Partie de Baptême

In the middle of the room is a simple pine table. It can easily seat eight butlers to polish and buff silver. It can also seat eight people for a party.

This early evening it seats only K. Burke and myself.

We sit facing each other. We sip a St. Emilion. The wine's château and vineyard names mean little to me and nothing to K. Burke.

Our moods are…well, I can only speak for me. I am slightly touched now with sadness, and yet I am happy that the process of the will has ended. Tomorrow is the funeral to get through, but then—after perhaps a day or two of shopping and museum-hopping—we will return to our favorite pastime—NYPD detective work.

We ignore the fruit and cheeses and charcuterie that the kitchen has assembled for us. We drink our wine.

Finally, Burke speaks.

"I see the newspaper headline now," Burke says. "Luc Moncrief, the Gloomiest Billionaire on Earth. Sob. Sob. Sob."

"K. Burke, surely you, of all people, are smart enough to know that a great big pot full of money does not make a person happy. Too many people in my position have jumped from skyscrapers, overdosed on drugs, murdered their lovers, died alone…money is a fine thing, especially if you do not have it, but it guarantees nothing other than money."

"Skip the lecture, Moncrief. Of course, I know all that. And I also know that your heart was broken into pieces when Dalia died. There's no amount in the world—no money, no work of art, no beautiful woman—who can repair that."

A pause, and then I say, "It is because of that wisdom that you and I are such fine friends."

"So, what's the problem, Moncrief? Is it just that your father has been good to you in death and that you wish that he had…"

"No. No. It is not the usual, not the obvious."

I decide to be blunt. I speak.

"I believe that my father was murdered."

Burke does not flinch. She barely reacts. Her eyes do not pop open. Her jaw does not drop. If anything she is a woman acting as if she's heard a very interesting piece of casual gossip.

"Hence, your one and only question to the attorney. The question about the doctor's report," she says.

"Of course. I knew you would deduce that."

"What makes you believe that…other than your impeccable instinct?" she asks.

"Sarcasm does not flatter you, K. Burke." I pause. Then I say, "Yes, it is my instinct, of course. But there are two small issues. *One,* my father was a man of great importance and great wealth. You know that the newspapers and political blogs referred to him as *le vrai président,* the real president. Surely the police and detectives would require an autopsy or some sort of medical investigation to assure that there was no foul play. That would be done for a cabinet minister or an ambassador's wife. But it was not done for one of the most important men in France? *Ridicule!*"

K. Burke takes a long gulp of her wine. She nods, but she says nothing. I have something else to add.

"Now, another thing, something perhaps a bit subtler, but not to be overlooked: Julien Carpentier mentioned innumerable times that my father died of a heart attack, that my father had heart disease, that my father passed painlessly because of the speed of his heart attack. How many times was it necessary to tell us that? Likewise, from Babette's very first phone call to me in the States, she too kept insisting that it was a heart attack, a heart attack, a heart attack. Dupain the attorney mentioned it.…Why so much attention to this? Yes, surely he may very well have died from a heart attack, but is it necessary to mention it so many times?"

I pour us more wine. Then Detective Burke lifts her purse from the floor. It is her big black leather satchel of a purse. She unzips the bag and puts her hand inside. She retrieves a business-sized envelope. It is cream-colored. It looks like fine heavyweight paper.

Burke hands the envelope to me. On the reverse side, just below my father's engraved initials, the envelope is held closed by a bit of red sealing wax.

"I found this envelope where I am staying, in your bedroom. It was leaning against the bronze inkstand on your desk. The envelope was meant to be discovered," she says.

I flip the envelope over. There, in my father's precise handwriting, are these words: *à mon fils*. To my son.

I grab a dinner knife from one of the bins. Then I slit the envelope open. I read the letter aloud.

My Dear Luc,

This letter assumes that you are now in Paris for my funeral, that you are in our house, in your former bedroom.

Here is what I wish you to know.

In April I received word from Julien Carpentier that our most important new product—Prezinol, a breakthrough treatment for childhood diabetes—was facing serious problems. Prezinol was to be my last great achievement. Valex had worked on it for decades.

Then this awful news arrived. Thirty percent of three hundred juvenile test volunteers in Warsaw suffered a dreadful reaction to the drug—kidney failure or stage one cancer of the liver.

Julien immediately (and without consulting me) dispatched a team of doctors to Poland. By the time Julien involved me in the matter, the doctors reported back that the kidney and liver damage were irreversible. They advised that we stop all testing immediately, and that we cancel our plans for a similar test in São Paulo.

I disagreed with this strategy. I could not allow Prezinol to fail. I posited that we might receive different results in São Paulo. I also knew from experience that it would take the Polish bureau of health a few months to take action against Valex.

I instructed Julien to proceed with everything as planned. He refused. In fact, he accused me of being—and I quote—"a senile old devil." He said that my entire life was driven by greed and ego.

The fact is this: Julien was correct. I realized the truth of his observation. It is one that you yourself had sometimes made.

That evening I instructed Julien to stop all testing in Warsaw, to cancel plans for the testing in São Paulo, and to arrange significant compensation for the Polish children who suffered such unspeakable damage.

I then considered what else I might do to compensate for my history of abhorrent behavior. Sadly I realized that there was no suitable punishment.

I realized I was just another old man with arthritis and heart disease. My financial success was everything and nothing.

I decided to address my situation as follows.

First, to name Julien as my successor at Valex. Julien has the skills and moral fiber to act in a way that will allow Valex to create pharmaceuticals that will advance worldwide health.

Second, to leave to you the vast portion of my wealth. Out

of guilt certainly for my years of paternal neglect, but also because you will use my fortune not merely to live well, but to live wisely.

Finally, to have delivered to me a shipment of fifty capsules of Prezinol.

My dear Luc, more than anything, I wish you the love I kept locked in my heart.

Votre père

CHAPTER 34

THE SONGWRITER WAS wrong when he wrote the lyrics that said he even loved "Paris in the winter, when it drizzles." I tell this to K. Burke as she and I walk the Boulevard Haussmann toward the enormous shopping cathedral known as Galeries Lafayette, after my father's funeral.

"The drizzle, it even gets through the finest wool coat," I complain.

"You should wear a good puffy ski jacket like mine," says Burke.

"I would rather wear a circus clown costume than a ski jacket."

"Say what you want, but I'm warm and dry, and you're cold and wet."

The morning had been a blur, but it was a mercifully short, respectful service with no gathering after. Except that I called Julien and Babette to meet with us. We ate homemade breakfast brioche and discussed my father's suicide.

Julien and Babette readily admitted that they knew the *full* story, and, yes, they had been complicit in hiding the method from me. They swore that they were going to tell me the truth and to put that truth "in context." That my father was suffering from advanced heart disease, that the children's diabetes drug had caused grave damage to many in the test group, that my father had, in fact, ended his own life by taking more than four dozen Prezinol capsules.

"We merely wanted to get through the funeral, Luc. With so many business matters and the will, it seemed like the right thing," Julien said. "I am sorry if we miscalculated."

I was inclined to believe him. I still am. You see, the simple truth is: What difference does it make? We move on. My father is gone. Babette is a sad old lady. Julien is set for a lifetime of overwhelming work. We move on. At least we try.

As for me, I am and will always be without my beloved Dalia. To have a death that meaningful in your life is to always have the tiniest cloud over even the greatest joy. My police work may fascinate me. Good friends like Burke will support me. France may win the World Cup. I may sip a magnificent Romanée-Conti. I may even fall in love again. Even that I cannot rule out. But: no matter. Dalia will not be here with me.

K. Burke and I continue our walk. Now we are within a block of the Galeries Lafayette. Christmas lights hang from the chestnut trees. Candles sit shining in the shop windows.

"You know, Moncrief. You're a real Frenchman," she says.

"Did you ever doubt it?" I ask.

"No. Here's why: you do what many Frenchmen do. I noticed. You don't walk. You *stroll.* Long strides, a little hip swing, head back. You're like a little cartoon of a French guy."

"There's a compliment hidden somewhere in those words, K. Burke. I just haven't found it yet."

So we stroll. We approach the Haussmann entrance to the store. Burke asks that we pause for a moment. We do, and she says, "So, you were right. Your instincts were true. Your father was murdered."

"But, of course not, K. Burke. Not murder. My father committed suicide."

"I guess, but…" she says. "He was a murderer who…murdered himself."

I tell Burke how I feel. That sometimes I believe his suicide was an old-fashioned noble gesture; that he had committed sins that could never be forgiven. So, *poof.* He punished himself.

"But then," I tell her, "I think he was an old-fashioned coward. The mere thought of *earthly* punishment—jail, humiliation—told him to escape. He up and left us. He left Babette, a woman who loved him. He left Julien, a young man who idolized him. And he left me, his son, the boy he barely knew, the man he *never* knew."

We walk inside the gilded department store. It looks like a Christmas tree turned upside down. Sparkle and glitter and thirty-feet-high gift boxes suspended from the vaulted ceiling. Burke looks upward, her neck stretching backward, as if she were standing in the Sistine Chapel. Her mouth literally opens in awe. The Christmas shoppers crowd the floor.

Then she says, "Let's start shopping before you start wanting to move on. I want to buy a few things to take back."

"I can assure you, K. Burke, there is almost nothing worth purchasing here."

"Well, thanks for the advice, Moncrief. But I think I'm about to prove that statement wrong."

I limit her, however, to one hour. In that short time she purchases a green Mark Cross Villa Tote bag, a pair of real silk stockings (the sort that also requires her to buy simple but quite intriguing garters), two tiny bronze replicas of the Arc de Triomphe (*"Vous touriste!"* I tell her), and four silk scarves (blue for her cousin Sandi, red for her cousin Elyce, yellow for her cousin Maddy, white for her cousin Marilyn). The scarves are my treat. I insist.

I also came out of the store with a purchase of my own. A five-pound tenderloin of venison.

"I shall give this venison to my father's cook, Reynaud, and you shall feast in a way you never have before."

"I'll say that it was interesting being in a butcher store inside a department store. But really…venison? Deer meat?"

"What is so odd about that?" I ask.

"I can tell you in one word: Bambi."

CHAPTER 35

I MUST ADMIT the truth: I am enjoying my day with K. Burke.

She is constantly refreshing, authentic. She has a complete honesty to her behavior. On the job she is not always charming, but here she always is. Burke is like a provincial schoolgirl on her first trip to Paris—wide-eyed and enthusiastic, but never irritating or vulgar. Burke has the purity that I have experienced in one other woman.

"We are going someplace really special now," I say.

"Galeries Lafayette was special enough for me," she says.

"Cease the humility, K. Burke. Where we are going next is…is almost…"

"*Incroyable?*"

"*Oui.* Almost unbelievable."

"It is only a short walk. It is on the Place Vendôme. But the drizzle is still drizzling. I'll try to get us a taxi."

"No, we'll walk," she says.

"But the rain. It is cold. It is icy."

"We'll walk."

So we walk, and I try to remember not to "stroll." K. Burke can't get enough of the Parisian excitement. Her head seems as if it's attached to a well-oiled fulcrum that allows her to snap her eyes from side to side in only a second.

We pass the furriers and jewelers and even the occasional hat store on our walk. Then, in front of a chocolate shop, of all places, I make a grave error.

"If there's anything you want, just say so, and we can get it," I say.

She stops walking. The smile leaves her face, and her head remains motionless.

"I don't want you to buy me anything…anything. I shouldn't have let you buy those expensive scarves for my cousins. I don't want *things*. Frankly, if you want to give me something, do it by giving *yourself* a gift…the gift of joy, some peace. What would truly make me happy is for you to be happy."

She brushes her cheeks with her hand, and I cannot be sure whether she is brushing away tears or merely brushing away the icy drizzle.

"You are a true friend, K. Burke," I say.

"I try to be," she says, her voice choking just a bit. "But it's hard to be a friend to a lucky man who has had some very bad luck."

"You are doing just fine," I say.

We continue our walk.

We are about to turn onto the Place Vendôme when she says, "By the way, Moncrief, you can stroll if you want to."

"I am walking slow because I am contemplating a problem," I say.

Burke looks nervous, serious.

"What's the matter?" she says.

"I have a problem that only you can solve."

"And that is?"

"That is this: we are going to a place where I had planned on purchasing you a combination Christmas–New Years–Friendship–Thank You gift. And now you say…" (I do a comic imitation of an angry woman) *"I don't want you to buy me anything!"*

"That's the problem?" she says.

"For me, that is a problem. Can you solve it?"

"Okay, *mon ami*. You may buy me one more thing. Just one. And then that's it."

CHAPTER 36

THE FLAG THAT is pinned over the doorway is not too big, not too small. It is surely not an elegant sign, although the small building itself is a beautifully designed nineteenth-century town house. The sign is wet from the rain, so it is wrinkled in many spots. Dark-purple letters—only three letters—are printed against a white background.

JAR

Quite logically K. Burke says, "Is it a store that sells jars? Or do the letters stand for something?"

"The letters stand for something," I say. "It is a man's name. Joel Arthur Rosenthal. He is the finest jeweler in the world, and, not surprisingly, he is here in Paris."

"Moncrief, when I said one more gift, I did not say jewelry. This is out of the question. I'm not going to allow…"

I put an index finger gently on her lips.

"I am going to ring the bell. I have an appointment. Let's try to keep our voices down."

Within seconds we are greeted by a very handsome young man

in gray slacks and a blue blazer. We exchange greetings in French, and then I introduce him to Detective Burke.

"*Mademoiselle Katherine Burke, je voudrais vous presenter Richard Ranftle,* the assistant to Monsieur Rosenthal."

"*Je suis enchanté, Mademoiselle.* I am also very much admiring of your coat. The North Face ski jacket has become everyone's favorite."

"*Merci, Richard,*" Burke says. Then she smiles at me.

"Monsieur Rosenthal regrets that he is not here to assist the both of you, but your phone call came only this morning, Monsieur Moncrief, and Monsieur Rosenthal had already left for his home in Morocco. He likes to escape Paris during the Christmas season."

A maid enters. She is dressed in full maid regalia—starched white cap, black dress, starched white apron with ruffle.

She asks if we would like tea or coffee or wine.

We decline.

"Perhaps some champagne," says Richard.

We decline again.

We follow Richard a few steps into what looks like the parlor of a small elegant apartment on the rue du Faubourg Saint-Honoré. A two-seat sofa in gray. A few mid-century wooden chairs with darker gray seats. A very bright crystal chandelier in the center of the ceiling. The only thing that distinguishes the room from a private residence are the four glass jewelry showcases.

Katherine Burke runs her hands along the glass enclosures. I watch her closely. We both seem to be nearly overwhelmed by the beauty of the jewels. Not merely the size of the diamonds but the un-usual designs of the bracelets and earrings and necklaces and rings.

"I know very little about jewelry, and it has been a few years since I have visited here, but these stones all seem to be enor-mous," I say.

"Joel…er, Monsieur Rosenthal, likes to work on a large canvas. You see, even when he uses small stones, as in a pavé setting, he sets them so close to one another that they look like a wall of dia-monds."

He points, as an example, to a ring with something called an "apricot" diamond at its center. The tiny diamonds around it look like a starry night.

Richard Ranftle shows us something called a "thread ring." If there were a piece of sewing thread composed of tiny diamonds, then flung into the air, then eventually landing in a messy heap, it would be this enormous ring. For good luck, Rosenthal seems to have decided that a very large amethyst should sit on top of this pile of extraordinary thread.

"Mademoiselle seems most interested in the rings, eh?" says Richard.

I note with amusement that Richard has perfected an amazing style. He is helpful without being condescending. He is courteous without being obnoxious. We are three people having fun. Million-dollar fun, but fun nonetheless.

Burke is slightly stoned, I think, on the jewelry on display.

"Look at that," she says, and she points to an enormous round green stone.

Richard immediately goes to work.

"It is a twelve-carat emerald. Monsieur Rosenthal was inspired to set the stone upside down. Then he surrounded it with a platinum and garnet rope. It is beyond nontraditional. He says it looks like 'a turtle from paradise.'"

Richard removes the ring from the glass case. He places it on a dark-purple velvet tray.

"Let me slip it onto your middle finger," says Richard. Then he pauses and says, "Unless you would care to do so, Monsieur Moncrief."

"No, no. Go right ahead," I say.

"My God," says Burke. "This is about the same size as my Toyota Camry."

"If you like, then, you can drive it out of the showroom," says Richard. We all smile.

She looks at the ring. She holds up her hand.

"I wish you'd told me we were coming here, Moncrief. I would have given myself a manicure."

The ring looks spectacular, huge and spectacular, beautiful and spectacular. I tell Burke to take it. She says, "Oh, no." I insist. She insists no. I say that it's a Christmas gift. She says this is ridiculous. I tell her that she promised I would be allowed to give her "just one gift." Then as an extra argument I say something that is probably not even true: "Look, Detective, how expensive can it be? It's only an emerald, not even a diamond."

For about three minutes the room remains completely silent. I do not know what is going through her head, of course. But when she finally speaks, she says, "Okay."

I smile. She smiles. Richard smiles. Richard hands me a small blue paper on which is written: "540,000 EU." I slip the paper into the wet pocket of my coat, and I continue to smile.

And that is how Detective Katherine Burke came to own the ring that came to be called "The Emerald Turtle."

CHAPTER 37

CHRISTMAS DAY IN PARIS is for family. Grand-père carving the goose. Grand-mère snoring from too much Rémy Martin. It is a day for children and chocolate.

I will not violate the spirit of the feast. Indeed, Reynaud, my late father's exceptional chef, will roast the tenderloin of venison. I have invited Babette and Julien and Julien's girlfriend, Anne. (Who knew Julien had a girlfriend? Who knew Julien had a life apart from Valex?)

So that will be Christmas Day. For Christmas Eve, however, I have made a special plan. Burke and I will have a night of fine dining.

"It will be a night perfect for wearing 'The Emerald Turtle,'" I say.

"I'm so nervous wearing it," says Burke. "If I lose it...if..."

"If you lose it, there are plenty more emeralds in the world," I say. "And if I sound like a spoiled rich kid, so be it. I am. At least for Christmas."

"I'm still nervous."

But, of course, she wears it.

The evening begins with—what else?—chilled Dom Pérignon in the warm and cozy backseat of the limo.

"Our first stop will be Les Ambassadeurs inside the Hôtel de Crillon," I tell K. Burke.

"Our *first* stop?" says Burke.

"*Oui*. The first course of seven courses," I say. "A different course at a different restaurant. I can imagine no finer way to welcome Christmas. This took much planning on my part."

We arrive at the Place de la Concorde. Five minutes later we are tasting artichoke soup with black truffle shavings. Exceptional.

Fifteen minutes later we are back in the car and headed for *le poisson,* the fish course. At L'Arpège my friend, Alain Passard, has prepared his three-hour turbot with green apples.

Just when we think nothing can surpass the turbot we move on to Lasserre. Here the magical dish is a delicate pigeon with a warm fig and hazelnut compote.

The maître d' at George V's Le Cinq describes a dish that both Burke and I think is ridiculous—a seaweed consommé with bits of turnip, parsnip, and golden beets floating on top. It is, of course, magnificent.

When we return to the car Burke announces, "I don't know how to say this properly. But I am full without really being full."

"You are *satisfied*," I say. "Small portions of exquisite food. The French never fill themselves. They eat. They think. They enjoy."

"Sure. That's it exactly," says K. Burke. Then, with a giggle in her voice, she says, "A bit more champagne, please."

The first four restaurants we have visited are classic Parisian restaurants. They have been filling famous bellies for many years—

royalty and food writers and a few pretentious snobs. But always the food has remained magnificent.

"Now we are going to have something completely modern," I tell my dining companion. "We are going to one of the famous new places that I call 'mish-mash-mosh' restaurants. You don't know whether you are eating Indian or French or Hungarian or Cambodian food. The classical chefs turn in their graves, but it is the future, and we must try one of them."

So Burke and I, a little tipsy from champagne and wine, sit at Le Chateaubriand, a fancy French name for a restaurant that looks like a 1950s American diner. The duck breast we are served is covered with fennel seeds and bits of…"What is this?" I ask the captain. He replies, "Tiny pieces of orange candy." This fabulous concoction sits next to a purée of strawberries that tastes a little bit of maple syrup, a little bit of tangerine.

K. Burke describes it perfectly: "It tastes like something wonderful, like something you'd get at a carnival in heaven."

"You have the vocabulary of a restaurant critic, K. Burke," I say.

We leave the heavenly carnival, and a short time later we are at Le Jules Verne, the foolishly named restaurant on top of the beloved *tour Eiffel*.

The alcohol is making me too happy, too giddy, and surely too talkative. "This is a restaurant that has maintained its integrity, even though it is in the very tourist heart of Paris," I say.

"I'm not ashamed to be a tourist," says Burke.

"Nor am I," I say. Then we sit down and look out at the marvel of Paris at night while we eat an impeccable piece of filet mignon—big beefy flavor in every meltingly tender bite.

"And now. On to dessert," I say.

"I should say 'I couldn't.' But the truth is…I could," Burke says.

"We will finish at my favorite place in all of Paris," I say. Soon our car is making its way through the narrow streets of the Marais.

All the chic little shops are closed. A small kosher restaurant is shutting down for the evening. "The best hummus in Europe," I say.

A few students are singing Christmas songs. They swig from open bottles of wine. Lights twinkle from many windows.

The car stops at a tiny corner shop on rue Vieille du Temple, very near the rue de Rivoli.

Burke reads the sign on the shop aloud, "Amorino." Then she says, "Whatever it is, it looks closed."

"Un moment," I say, and I hit a few numbers on my phone. *"Nous sommes ici."* We are here. A young woman appears at the shop door. She is smiling. She gestures to us. We go inside.

"It's an ice cream parlor," Burke says.

"Yes and no. It is a gelato shop. When I lived in Paris—before moving to New York—no evening was complete unless we had a two-scoop chocolate and amaretto cone at Amorino. What flavors do you like? The pistachio is magnificent."

She looks away from me. When she faces me again she is blinking her eyes.

"Would you think I'm rude if I skip the gelato?" she says.

"But you would love it," I say.

"It's been a great evening. I appreciate it. I really do," she says. "But I've had enough."

Then it hits my thoughtless French brain. Suddenly, as if a big rock fell on my stupid little head.

"Oh, K. Burke. I am sorry. I am awful and stupid. I am sorry."

"You have nothing to be sorry about," she says. "It was a wonderful night. It is a beautiful ring. This is the nicest Christmas I've ever had."

Then I find the courage to say what I should say.

"Forgive me, Katherine. I gave you a night of glamour without the romance that should accompany it. Forgive me." She smiles at me.

"There's nothing to forgive, Moncrief. You're terrific. You're the best friend I've ever had."

EPILOGUE

NEW YEAR'S EVE
NEW YORK CITY

IF I REALLY wanted to stretch the truth, I could say that my partner K. Burke and I are spending New Year's Eve at the Plaza Hotel. But as I say, that would be stretching the truth. A lot.

The fact is, the two of us are spending New Year's Eve in the underground loading alley under the kitchens of the Plaza Hotel.

It seems that our boss, Inspector Nick Elliott, wanted to bring us back to reality after our time in Paris. So Burke and I are on a drug stakeout in the repugnant, disgusting garbage zone beneath the fancy hotel. We are waiting for a potential "chalk drop." That's cop-talk for a major delivery of methamphetamine, a fairly wicked drug for some of the New Year's Eve revelers.

The smell of garbage, the whip of the winter wind, and the knowledge that most of New York is dancing the night away does nothing to relieve our boredom. And as with most stakeouts, the boredom is excruciating.

"So this is how it goes, right, Moncrief?" Burke says. "A week ago we were on top of the Eiffel Tower. Tonight we're in a hole under the Plaza."

I laugh and say, "That's life. Even for a rich kid." I pause for a moment as I watch a rat scurry past us. Then I say, "You know,

K. Burke, the truth is, I am enjoying this surveillance routine al-most as much as—but not *quite* as much as—our Christmas Eve in Paris. Simply put, I love doing detective work. Can you believe that?"

She does not hesitate. She says, "Yes, Moncrief. I can believe that."

Before I can even smile there is a great eruption of firecrackers and noisemakers and the noise of people shouting with joy.

"Listen closely, Moncrief. You can hear the music," Burke says.

She is right. From somewhere inside the hotel the orchestra is playing "Auld Lang Syne."

I lean in and kiss her on her cheek.

"Happy New Year, K. Burke," I say.

She leans in and kisses me on *my* cheek.

She speaks.

"Happy New Year, my friend."

CHAPTER 1

MY MOODY MONGREL, Bart Simpson, kept watch from the warm back-seat. He rarely found my job interesting. At least not this job.

I was next to the loading dock, folding newspapers for delivery. A surly driver named Nick dropped them off for me every morning at 5:50 sharp. What he lacked in personality he made up for in silence. I always said hello and never got an answer. Not even a "Hey, Mitchum." It was a good working relationship.

Even with the wind off the Hudson, I could crack a sweat moving the heavy bundles of papers. I used the knife I had gotten in the Navy to cut the straps holding them. My station wagon sagged under the weight of a full load. My two-day-a-week afternoon gig in Milton didn't strain the shocks nearly as bad. I usually dropped Bart off at my mom's then. My dog was as close to a grandchild as she had, and they could both complain about me.

In the early morning gloom, I caught a movement out of the corner of my eye and reacted quickly, turning with the knife still in my right hand. It was an instinct I couldn't explain. I was raised in upstate New York, not Bosnia. But I relaxed as soon as I saw Albany Al, one of the few homeless people in Marlboro, standing near the loading dock, a dozen feet away.

The older man's whiskers spread as he grinned and rubbed his hand across his white beard. "Hello, Mitchum. They say you can never sneak up on a Navy SEAL. I guess that's true."

I was past the point of explaining to people that I was never an actual SEAL.

When I took a closer look at the old man, I realized he wasn't ready for the burst of arctic air that had descended on us. "Al, grab my extra coat from the car. It's too cold to be wandering around dressed like that."

"I couldn't."

"Go ahead. My cousin usually wears it, but she didn't show today. She's a wuss for avoiding the cold."

"I wondered where Bailey Mae was. I was hoping she had some of her coffee cake."

Then I realized the older man hadn't come to keep me company. He'd wandered over to snag some of Bailey Mae's famous coffee cake, which she handed out like business cards.

I said, "I miss her cake, too."

The old man said, "I can tell." He cackled as he rubbed his belly, but he was looking at me.

I patted my own belly and said, "It's my portable insulation." Maybe I hadn't been working out as hard as usual. A few warm days and some running would solve that.

The old man continued to cackle as he walked away with my coat.

CHAPTER 2

WHEN I'D FINISHED my route, I headed over to my office off Route 9. At least, my unofficial office. I always hit Tina's Plentiful at about 8:15, right between the early breakfast crowd and late risers. The old diner sat in an empty strip mall that hadn't been updated since 1988. A couple of framed posters of the California coast hung on the walls. No one had ever explained their significance, and none of the customers seemed to care. The place had the best Reubens and tuna melts in upstate New York, and they treated me like family. Maybe it was because one of my cousins worked in the kitchen.

The lone waitress, Mabel, named by a mean-spirited mother, lit up when I walked in. Usually I sat in the rear booth to eat and see if I had any pressing business. There was never much pressing in Marlboro. Today I headed toward the counter since there wasn't much going on and it would make it easier on Mabel.

Mabel was a town favorite for her easy smile and the way she took time to chat with everyone who came into the diner. As soon as I sat down she said, "Finally, a friendly face."

I gave her a wink and said, "Is the world not treating Miss Teenage New York well today?"

"Funny. You should cheer me up by taking me to the movies in Newburgh one night."

"Only if my cousin Bailey Mae comes with us."

"Why?"

"So you understand it's as friends and not a date."

"Am I so terrible? You've had some tough breaks and I'm a lot of fun."

I couldn't help a smile. "Of course you're not so terrible. You're also so *young*. And I'm not going to be the guy who holds you back from all the suitable young men in the area." That was as much as I wanted to say today.

Before she could answer, I glanced out the wide front window and saw my cousin Alice, Bailey Mae's mom, hustling across the street toward the diner. She is a year older than me and was only twenty when Bailey Mae was born. She is a good mom, and the rest of us help. Her usual smile was nowhere to be seen as her long brown hair flapped in the wind behind her. She yanked open the door and rushed right to me.

"Mitchum, Bailey Mae is missing."

Suddenly, the day got colder.

ABOUT THE AUTHORS

JAMES PATTERSON has written more bestsellers and created more enduring fictional characters than any other novelist writing today. He lives in Florida with his family.

RICHARD DiLALLO is a former advertising creative director. He has had numerous articles published in major magazines. He lives in Manhattan with his wife.

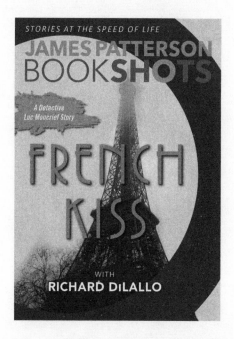

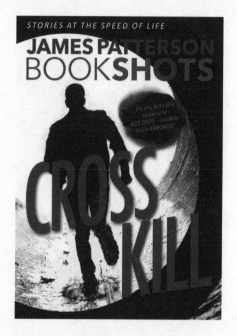